THE JANUARY CORPSE

A Dave Garrett Mystery

Neil Albert

Dedicated to Evelyn Albert
My wife and so much more

Also in the Dave Garrett Series

CHAPTER ONE
Friday, 11:00 A.M.

I couldn't stand the sight of him but I took his case anyway. I'd been sitting in the spectator's section of a courtroom in the basement of the Court of Common Pleas of Philadelphia County. At night the room was used for criminal arraignments, and it showed. Everything in the room was dirty, even the air. I breathed in a mixture of grit, poverty and despair. The bare wooden benches were carved in complex, overlapping swirls of graffiti, initials, gang emblems, and phone numbers. Some people called it street art. I didn't. To my left, fifteen feet off the ground, a clock was built into the wall. It was missing its hands and most of the brass numerals, and the few that were left were muddy brown. Not that I cared what time it was; as long as I sat there, waiting to testify, my meter was running.

Today the room was being used by the Family Court for a custody case. This was the second day of trial, and the wife's attorney was hoping to get me on the stand today. There's no such thing as a custody case with class. The couple were both doctors, both well respected. Married ten years, two children, both girls, ages four and seven. They had separated two years ago. Each had a condo; his was just south of Society Hill in a newly gentrified neighborhood; hers was on Rittenhouse Square. They both had memberships at the usual country clubs, plus time-shares in Aspen and Jamaica. She drove a BMW and he drove a Benz. It had been amicable at first. Neither one was leaving for someone else; they just didn't like being married to each other anymore. There was no one stirring it up. Most spouses need encouragement from a third

2

party to get really nasty--a new girlfriend, a mother, a friend, or a lawyer. In the absence of someone to stir the pot, it was very civilized. For a while. Then, while working out a property settlement, her lawyer found that her husband had forgotten to disclose his half-interest in a fast-food franchise--a small matter of half a million dollars. In response, she dropped the blockbuster; she moved to terminate his visitation rights because she claimed he was sexually abusing the seven-year-old. He denied it and countered with a suit for attorney's fees and punitive damages. The case had started yesterday, was being tried again today, and would probably go on for a good chunk of the next two weeks.

I had very little to say, but the wife's lawyer wanted me to testify anyway. In a close case, almost anything might make a difference. I'd followed the husband for a week, and the most interesting thing I'd found was that he read *Penthouse*. Plus, as I was sure his lawyer would point out on cross, *Time, Sports Illustrated, Business Week,* and *The New England Journal of Medicine.*

The wife's attorney, sitting at counsel table, turned to me, pointed to his watch, and shook his head. The cross examination of the wife's child psychologist was hopelessly bogged down on the question of her credentials, and they weren't going to reach me that day. The case wasn't on again until the following Wednesday; I was free till then. I nodded, pointed to my own watch to indicate that my meter was off and headed for the door. My overcoat was already over my arm; no one familiar with the Court of Common Pleas of Philadelphia County leaves their property unattended. There used to be a sign outside the Public Defender's office: Watch your hat, ass, and overcoat, till somebody stole it. The corridor was as filthy as the courtroom, but at least there was light. And people-- lots of them. The young and shabbily dressed ones were there for misdemeanor criminal or for family law cases. The felony defendants were usually older and better dressed; they'd learned the hard way that making a good impression just might help. The best dressed of all--except for the big-time drug defendants, who put everyone to shame--were the civil trial attorneys. There was big money in personal injury work and large commercial claims, and a lot of it was worn on their backs. My own suit, when it was new, had looked like theirs; now it was dated and worn, and my tie had a small stain. I was dressed well enough for what I did now.

I was nearly to the exit, feeling blasts of cold air as people went in and out, when I heard him call my name. The voice was raspy and nasal. I turned; it was Mark Louchs, a classmate from law school. He practiced with a small firm out in the suburbs. His hairline had receded since I'd last seen him, and he was wearing new, thicker glasses. His skin was red, probably from a recent Caribbean vacation. He smiled, shook my hand, and said he was so glad to see me. It was all too fast and too hearty, and I wondered what he wanted from me.

"Hello, Mark. Going well for you?"

"God, hearings coming out my ears. Clients calling all hours. Can't get away from it. My accountant—I'm busy as hell--" He stopped himself. "Yeah. Fine. Look, you know how bad I feel about what happened to you." His voice trailed off. He'd been a jerk when I needed his help and we both knew it. I said nothing, letting the awkward silence go on. Making him uncomfortable was petty, but that didn't stop me from enjoying it. When he was nervous, I noticed, his smile was a little lopsided.

When he was certain that I was going to leave him hanging, he went on. "Look, I hear you're doing investigations now."

"It's the closest thing I can do to keep my hand in. And I sure wasn't going to hang around as somebody's research assistant."

"I tried to reach you first thing this morning. They said you were out."

I hadn't had time to check my messages, but I just stayed quiet. I liked leaving him under the impression that I was in no hurry to talk to him. Partly because it might give me an advantage in whatever he wanted with me, and partly because it was true.

"Listen, Dave, I'd like you to do me a favor. Are you set up to handle a rush job?"

I do plenty of favors, but not in business. And not for someone who didn't respond to my request for a letter of support when I'd

4

gone before the Disciplinary Board with my license on the line. I kept my voice disinterested and cautious.

"How much a favor, and how much a rush?"

"I need you to do an investigation for a case to be heard this coming Monday at one thirty."

I carefully gave a low whistle, watching for his reaction.

"That gives me just the rest of today and the weekend. Pretty short notice."

"If you can do it, the fee should be no problem. I'm sure we can agree on an acceptable rate."

I looked at his suit and at my own. I knew the money would never wind up in a suit. I had too many other bills. But it gave me something to focus on.

"Let's go somewhere and hear about it."

We put on our overcoats, cut through the perpetual construction around City Hall and wound up at a small bar near Sansom. He found a quiet corner booth and ordered two coffees. Whatever serious lawyers do after five, they don't drink during the day.

"Ever do a presumption of death hearing?" he asked.

"Fifteen years ago, fresh out of law school, I did a memo for a partner."

"Familiar with the law?"

"Unless it's changed. If all you have is a disappearance, no body or other direct proof of death, the passage of seven years without word gives rise to a presumption of death. If the person were alive, the law assumes that someone would have heard from them."

"I represent the survivors of a man who disappeared under circumstances strongly suggestive of his death. His name is—was-- Daniel Wilson. We filed an action to have him declared dead. The hearing is Monday afternoon at one-thirty in Norristown. The insurance company is fighting tooth and nail."

"What carrier? I do some work for USF&G and for Travelers. I'd hate to get on their bad side."

"Neither of them. Some one-lung life insurance outfit out of Iowa. Reliant Fidelity Mutual, or something like that."

"Let's hear some more."

"He lived in Philly and had offices in the city and in Norristown. I figured that his office in Norristown gave me enough to get venue in Montgomery County. I don't come into Philadelphia for trials if I can avoid it. The insurance company won't offer a nickel, but they don't care if it's in Philadelphia or Montgomery County."

"What kind of office?"

"A law office. Never heard of the guy before this case, though. I made a couple calls to friends from law school, but neither of them knew him."

"Lawyers aren't disappearing kinds of people. We're more like barnacles."

"Wait till you hear about the disappearance. Just after New Year's, seven years ago. His sister was in town from LA; they planned to get together. They're in separate cars, out in the country. Powell Township, Berks County. She finds his car off the road full of bullet holes. Plenty of blood, but no body. Police can't turn up shit. He was never heard from again."

It was short notice, but I had no plans for the weekend. It sounded like a break from skip traces and catching thieving employees. And it paid.

"The case has been kicking around for months. You didn't decide to hire an investigator this morning."

Even in the dimness I could tell he was flustered.

"Yeah, you're right; you're getting sloppy seconds. The Shreiner Agency was handling it till yesterday."

I just sat there until he decided to continue." They were doing all the usual interviews, credit checks, asset checks. They hand-delivered back the file and refunded our retainer. And a letter saying they wouldn't be able to help any further."

"Someone warned them off."

"There could be other reasons."

"This thing smells to me like organized crime. That's out of my league."

"Look, nobody's asking you to find who killed him, even if he's dead. We just need to say that there's no evidence he's alive.

That ought to be easy enough. He didn't say the words 'even for you', but I heard them.

"Tell that to the Shreiner Agency."

He finished his coffee. He was anxious to get help, but I was clearly hitting a nerve.

"Yes or no?"

I normally worked for a flat fifty dollars an hour. Right then, considering who I'd be working for and whatever had happened to the Shreiner Agency, I wasn't so sure if I wanted it.

"I charge my attorney's rate--one hundred fifty per hour; two hundred for work outside of business hours, half rate for travel time, plus all expenses."

"Think you can come up with something for that kind of money?"

"Haven't the slightest idea. You know how it is. I work by time, not results."

"That's a lot of money."

"And it's quarter to twelve on Friday."

He gave me the kind of look I didn't normally associate with being hired--it was closer to the expression you get when you steal somebody's parking place. But he grunted something that sounded like "okay" and gave me his business card with his home number on it. And the Shreiner file, too--there was so little of it, he was carrying it in his breast pocket.

"I'll look this over and do what I can this afternoon. When can I talk to the sister?" I asked.

"Give me your card. She's in the area. I'll have her at your office at nine tomorrow morning."

"Make it seven; I don't want to lose any time on Saturday. It's tougher to reach people on Sunday."

"Okay, but keep me posted, will you? Remember that you're working under the supervision of an attorney."

"Right." I wanted to tell him that I was working under the supervision of an asshole, but I let it pass.

Philadelphia has mild winters, but early January is no time to linger outside. I needed a quiet place to read. I went to Suburban Station and found an empty bench.

The Shreiner Agency was like the Army: bloated, bureaucratic, and sluggish, and most of its best people moved along after a few years. Yet they were careful and scrupulously honest. That counted for a lot in my business.

The file was only about twenty pages, and most of it was negative information. Daniel Wilson hadn't voted in his home district since the time of his disappearance. Neither had he started any lawsuits, mortgaged any real estate, filed for bankruptcy, used his credit cards, joined the armed forces, opened any bank accounts, or taken out a marriage license. His driver's license had expired a year after he disappeared and had never been renewed. At the time of his disappearance he had no points on his license and no criminal record. Since then, there had been no activity in his checking or savings accounts; the balances in each were a few hundred dollars. No income taxes or property taxes bad been paid in seven years. None of this distinguished Daniel Wilson from somewhere between ten and fifteen percent of the population. I would need a lot more than this to convince a judge he was dead.

Toward the bottom of the pile I found an interim report by "JBF" who I knew to be Jonathan Franklin, an investigator I'd worked with before. According to the report, at the time of his disappearance Wilson was thirty years old, short to medium height, wiry build, brown hair and eyes. Paper-clipped to the corner of the first page was a black-and-white wallet-size formal photo of Wilson in a suit and tie. From the date on the back, it was probably his law school graduation portrait. Assuming he graduated at twenty-five, the picture was twelve years old. I had visions of showing it and asking people if they'd ever seen an average-looking guy with glasses and brown hair before. It was a pleasant-looking face; maybe a little bland, but presentable. His cheeks were smooth and pink, and he looked closer to twenty than twenty-five.

His glasses weren't the wire-rimmed ones that were fashionable when I was in college, or the high-tech rimless models the yuppies wore now, but good old-fashioned ones, horn rimmed, with a heavy frame. He had the kind of face clients would trust.

The family background was minimal. Wilson's father had died when he was a child; his mother was still living and worked cleaning offices in Center City. She lived in the Overbrook section of west Philadelphia. There was one sibling, a sister, Lisa, two years older; a former nurse who now lived in a small town upstate. She'd been living in LA, if I remembered Louchs correctly. I figured her for a loyal daughter who'd moved back east to be close to their mother after Daniel's death, or disappearance, or whatever it was. Neither Lisa nor Daniel had any children. Neither had ever been married.

Franklin had come up with some more about Wilson's grade and high school education. Wilson was consistently a superior student; not brilliant, but always near the top of the class. He was seldom absent, hardly ever late with work assignments, and never a discipline problem. Several of his high school classmates had been contacted; they remembered him as serious and hardworking. He played no sports but was active with the school literary magazine and the newspaper.

He had a few dates, but no one remembered a steady girlfriend.

Except to tell me that he'd attended Gettysburg College, was secretary of the Photography Club, and obtained a degree in history, the college section was a blank. I wasn't surprised; in high school everybody knows everybody. But people are too busy in college to know more than a couple of people well. Investigating backgrounds at the college level is usually helpful only if the subject was very well known or if the school was very small. I was reading with only half my attention by then; I was trying to imagine what kind of man was behind that picture. And what was the judge going to make of him.

I hoped he wouldn't decide that Wilson was the kind of loner who would pull up stakes and disappear without a word to anybody.

The next section was hardly more help. After college, three years at Temple Law School, graduating about one-third of the way from the top. He passed the bar on the first try and set up practice in

Center City with a classmate, Leo Strasnick. When Wilson disappeared five years later, the partnership already had three associates, with offices in Philadelphia and Norristown. Nice growth. I rubbed my eyes and looked at my watch. It was nearly one, and this was the only business day before the day of the hearing. The rest of the file would have to wait.

One of the advantages of Suburban Station was plenty of phone booths. My investigation got off on the right foot. Not only was Leo Strasnick available, he agreed to see me at four that afternoon. His office was only a few blocks from the station.

I tried Shreiner's next.

"Shreiner Security Agency. How may we help you?" She sounded like a recording of herself.

"Mr. Franklin, please."

"And whom may I say is calling?" She was good. If my gross ever broke into seven figures, I promised myself I would get a receptionist who talked that well. And to take lessons from her.

"Just say I'm calling regarding the Wilson case." I was curious to see if that would be enough to get me through.

"Yeah, this is Jon Franklin," was all he said, but it was enough. Something was bothering him. His words were unnaturally clipped, and his voice was too loud and too fast.

"Hello, Jon, this is Dave Garrett—"

"You said you were calling about Wilson?"

"Yeah, right," I said as casually as I could "Remember me, Jon? We worked together on those tools disappearing out of Sun Shipbuilding? I was—"

"I remember." Then his voice got softer. "Dave, what do you have to do with this? We're not in the Wilson case."

"I've just taken it over."

There was silence on the other end.

"I've read your report and I assume there's more than you had time to put in writing."

More silence.

"Look, Jon, the case is coming up Monday, for Christ's sake. Cut me some slack."

"You want some advice? Don't take the case."

"The lawyer guaranteed payment," I said, being deliberately stupid. I had a lot of practice at that.

"No amount of money is worth it."; I'd been expecting him to say that, but he was at the biggest agency in the state a fifteen-year veteran of the Philadelphia police.

"Can we get together somewhere?"

"I've told you all you need to know already," he said, and hung up.

CHAPTER TWO
Friday, 1:00 P.M.

Suburban Station was dirty, and the air was stale, but at least it was warm. By the time I'd walked a few blocks in the wind I was missing it.

To do the investigation right I should have started at the end-- seen the site, reviewed the evidence, and talked to the police. Once I decided if I was dealing with a homicide, an accident, a suicide, or a disappearance, I would know what to look for. But there was only time enough to scramble around and work as fast as I could, hoping to turn up something.

With a little luck, I would find a pattern. Without any luck, I'd be on the witness stand Monday in my best suit, with a set, all-business expression on my face, and my dick in my hand while a lawyer from the insurance company made me look like an idiot. My luck hadn't been very good in the last few years.

The last place Wilson called home was only about half a mile away. I caught a bus going up the Ben Franklin Parkway, got off just before the Art Museum, and walked. Years ago, before the Depression, Wilson's old neighborhood had been the southern boundary of the old Jewish area of north Philly. Then a few black families started moving in and the whites fled north, fighting a twenty-year delaying action as they retreated up Broad Street. No Russian general ever surrendered space for time as skillfully. Finally, they succeeded in barricading themselves in the Northeast section by blocking the planned northern expansion of the subway system. Now their sons and daughters were moving back south again. Who wanted to be stuck way out in the Northeast with no subway?

The area surrounding the Art Museum had been attracting attention for years, ever since Society Hill became a hundred percent gentrified. Now it was at a tipping point, about one-tenth abandoned row houses and two-tenths expensive townhouse condos. The rest of the area was trying to make up its mind. Construction signs evidenced the hopes and greed of real estate brokers, banks, and contractors.

I turned onto his old block and tried to imagine how it must have looked when he lived there. It wasn't hard. Almost all the houses were darkened with an undisturbed hundred-year layer of soot. Some windows were flanked by pale rectangular patches of black where shutters had once been attached. Except for a pink-and-green corner grocery store, the block was mostly three-story brick row houses with small concrete porches. Every first floor and basement window had iron bars, and most of the doors had multiple locks. Some nice cars were parked on the street, the kinds that cost as much as houses used to, but they didn't look like they belonged there. The license plates announced dealerships in Chestnut Hill and King of Prussia; I assumed they belonged to yuppies who worked in offices on the Parkway and didn't want to spend fifteen dollars a day for garage parking. The cars that looked like they belonged there were old and tired, like the houses.

Wilson's old address was a converted row house with three apartments, separated from its neighbor to the east by a narrow alley. No one answered any of the buzzers. The side of the building was covered with graffiti to a height of six feet. Some car tires and a rusted bicycle frame protruded from the rest of the rubbish in the small backyard.

I looked around; no one was on the street. The time of year to do this sort of work was in the summer when people are out. Every city neighborhood had people who sit out on their porches and watch what goes on: housewives, retirees, the disabled. But none of them were crazy enough to be outside in twenty degrees with a brisk wind. The light coating of snow crunched under my feet. I kept my head down, looking for patches of ice. The concrete sidewalk was in poor shape; too many tree roots and garbage, and not enough care.

I tried two houses before I could even get anyone to answer the door, and three more after that where they'd never heard of Wilson. The cold was seeping around the buttons of my coat and cutting through my suit right to my skin. I decided to try a run-down three-story apartment building directly across the street, and if that didn't work, I would give up my visit as a bad idea.

The front door opened into a small alcove. Beyond it was an oak door with carved trim, set with a big pane of glass with beveled edges. This building has seen better days, a long time ago. Through the glass I could see a dim hallway with red carpeting. There were five buzzers in the alcove; one had no name next to it and none of the other four answered. That's what you get, I told myself, for coming around in the middle of a weekday.

I was putting on my gloves again when I saw movement in the hallway. I tapped on the glass and a short black man, about sixty, opened the door. His remaining fringe of hair was gray, and an unlit cigar hung in the corner of his mouth. His right eye was covered by a black eye patch.

"Hi, my name is Dave Garrett. I'm looking for someone who used to live around here."

He pursed his lips and nodded thoughtfully; about what I couldn't imagine. But he held the door wider and motioned me inside.

"Thanks. It's a lot warmer in here."

"It's a cold one." His voice was soft and tired, like good blues late at night.

"The fellow I'm looking for lived across the street until seven years ago. You live around here then?"

"The wife and I moved in here when I came back from Korea, after I got outta the hospital." He said "Korea" with the emphasis on the first syllable.

"The guy's name is Dan Wilson. He was a lawyer." I wasn't sure whether to talk about him in the past tense or the present. I showed the little picture, for what it was worth.

"Average height, a little on the short side, brown hair, clean-shaven, glasses, about thirty the last time he was seen."

"Now who you say you was?"

"I'm an investigator. His family hired me to try and find out what happened to him. He disappeared seven years ago, and no one's heard from him since."

"Family hired you?"

"Yes, sir."

"Well, I knew him. Met his momma, too. She said he was dead."

"I know that's what she thinks," I said, lying just a little.

"And it may be true, for all I know." That part, at least, was the truth. "There's a court case coming up to declare him legally dead." Since he seemed interested in Wilson's family, I went a little further. "The case allows his money can be distributed to his heirs. I'm supposed to find out what I can about what happened."

His voice was still soft, but it was less tired. "Well, now. I understand that. Yeah, I can talk to you 'bout him." He didn't invite me into his apartment, but the hallway would suit me fine. I could feel my pulse pick up. I had a witness and I was out of the wind. I was talking to somebody who knew him, somebody who had nothing to hide. Somebody who Shreiner hadn't talked to. There were possibilities.

I got out a small notebook. I had a pocket tape recorder, but I left it in my briefcase; sometimes it makes people freeze up. "That'd be great if you could give me a couple of minutes, Mister . . ."

"Harrison. Gerald Harrison."

"How well did you know him?"

"Oh, let's see. He lived there a couple of years, I guess. I seen him comin'. I got the apartment here in the front, I looked out at his front door, and I saw him more days than not. I'm home all day. He wasn't in a hurry we'd wind up talkin' for a few minutes, most nights, if I was sitting on the stoop. Helped me dig my car outta the snow a couple times. I got a bad back; VA disability pension. Hurt in combat, you know. At the Pusan perimeter." Again he emphasized the first syllable, but for all I knew, that was how to pronounce it. He'd been there. "Seemed like a nice young fella. Even though he was a lawyer and all, he wasn't too busy for other folks, you know."

"Were you ever inside his place?"

"Not when he lived there. But after."

"Huh?"

"His momma come down and cleaned out his place right after he died. She said he was killed by some gangsters. I saw her carrying stuff out. I never met her before, but she seemed to be in a big hurry, and I sorta noticed that and I goes over. She was no kid and I felt sorry she was working so hard. We started talkin'. She asked, could she hire me to help move the stuff? So I did. But I wouldn't take no money for it. She needed the help, and he was a nice boy."

"Tell me what was inside."

"She'd been working before I ever got in there, a lot of stuff was already packed up in boxes. There was his personal stuff, you know, clothes, papers, books, dishes and things. We loaded all that in her car. She said it was going to the Salvation Army. I packed up the furniture, books, the rest of his clothes, everything else."

"Where did it go?"

"She borrowed a little van from somebody. I didn't ask. I suppose it went to the Salvation Army, too. Except the books; the Public Library sent a truck around for them."

"What kind of books?"

"All kinds. College books. Law books. You could tell from talkin' to him, he was a reading man, and Lord he was. Lots of travel books. And picture books."

"What kind of pictures?"

"Books about picture taking. Photography. He was a real good picture taker. Took pictures of my grandchildren one time. Real nice pictures, too.

"Did he have many visitors?"

"Well, the ladies." His good eye sparkled a little. He had been married to the same women for forty years.

"Tell me about them."

"Oh, I seen some. He was a young fellow, not bad looking, had a good job . . . A couple I only saw one time. But there was one blonde lady, with long hair; curly, you know, she was around a lot and she spent the night. Named Elizabeth. I remember her because that's my granddaughter's name. Nice lady. He even introduced me."

A steady girlfriend who was with him near the end.
She might not know everything, but she had to know something.

"Do you remember her last name?"

"No. I'm sure sorry."

"Nobody expects you to. It's been a long time. Can you tell me anything else about her?"

"Just that she seemed nice. And she dressed well. They held hands a lot."

Every case had dead ends. You got used to it.

"You said there were others?"

"Well, a couple. He was mainly with the blonde woman.
A couple of them I only saw once or twice. But there was the other lady I saw. She came and went without him. Either she had a key, or he left one for her with somebody."

"Can you describe her?"

"I never saw her close up; only across the street. About his age. She had blond hair; but not long like Elizabeth's. Real nice figure. Not too broad and not too narrow, if you know what I mean. And she knowed how to move it, too. Long legs, and she usually wore high heels. Fine lookin' woman. She wore good clothes, but not like the other lady. I mean, Elizabeth wore goin'-to-work clothes. This other lady wore, like, out-on-the-town clothes."

"You mean, sexier clothes?"

"Yes, sir." He didn't say anything more. He wasn't going to discuss his observations about sexy-looking white women with a strange white man. I was momentarily startled; while we were talking I hadn't been conscious of his color. A white person has the luxury of forgetting the race of the person he's talking to. Whoever this woman was, she knew things Elizabeth didn't.

"Did you get her name?"

"We was never introduced. I never spoke to her. She just came and went."

"When his mother was there, did you ever meet his sister?" I looked at my notes. "Her name is Lisa and she was a nurse."

"No, sir."

From what I knew of the file, it sounded like the woman might be Wilson's sister anyway. Or any one of the quarter of a million young blondes in Philadelphia, all of whom had either turned me down already or would do so in the future.

"Can you tell me anything else about these women?"

"I didn't pay close attention," he insisted.

Like hell you didn't, I wanted to say, but I wasn't going to argue with a source of information, no matter if it turned out to be useful or not.

"Did he have any male friends?"

"Sometimes, somebody'd visit. A couple of times some men his age dropped him off. But not often. He never had no parties or anything like that."

"What did he do with his time?"

"When he wasn't working, I don't know. He was gone a lot. Travelin," he said.

"Where did he travel?" He wouldn't be the first person who liked one of his destinations so much he decided to stay.

"He didn't say. He said he was doin' a lot of traveling on weekends when he wasn't working. Like up to New York or upstate looking at them small towns."

"Did he go alone, or did he take Elizabeth?"

"I don't know. Wasn't my business. I never actually seen him leave or get back. His car would be gone at funny times and then just be there again."

"Funny times?"

"Like, he'd leave and come back in the middle of the night, like take off Friday midnight and come back early Monday morning.

Or leave real early Saturday morning and come back late Sunday night."

"Any reason you can think of for that?"

"No, sir. 'Cept he was young and single. He could come and go as he pleased."

I was getting tired. Talking to Harrison was like opening a treasure chest, over and over, and each time finding just rocks. A last name, a couple of details, and this could have been worthwhile.

"You think of anything else I'd appreciate it if you'd give me a call." I handed him a card. "You can call anytime. If I'm not there you can leave a message on the answering machine." I thought of giving him ten dollars for his time, and then decided against it. He might be old and beat up and not able to chase women as well as he used to, but he had his pride. Instead, I spent ten minutes asking about his service days on the Pusan perimeter.

I headed back toward the Parkway and stopped for a hot dog from a pushcart vendor. Even though it was mid-afternoon, there was a line. Everyone ahead of me was wearing an overcoat over a suit and tie. That's another funny thing about Philadelphia: It isn't a town that stops to eat during the day. If you want a two-hour business lunch, go to New York. You can walk around Center City on a nice day and see the business and professional people eating hot dogs and sausages and gulping down cans of soft drinks.

Almost all of them are standing up, and most are walking while they eat. In the Seventies, one of the local TV stations even had a regular show called "Sidewalk Gourmet," with tips on the best pushcarts. It boosted the station's ratings five percent.

Since I was on a case, I splurged--not only an Italian sausage, but coffee and a soft pretzel, too. With mustard, of course. By the time I finished my coffee the weather didn't seem so cold. I checked my watch; I still had some time left, so I decided to play a long shot. The report from Shreiner's said that Wilson had banked at the First Pennsylvania Bank. There was a branch across the street, just visible on one of the little side streets, only a couple of blocks from

Wilson's apartment. He could have banked over in Center City, near the courthouse and his office, but the local branch was worth a try.

When I stepped inside I decided it might not be such a long shot after all. It was a step back into the nineteenth century: heavy furniture, brass chandeliers, and dark wood paneling. Almost every lawyer has a sense of history; it's the nature of the profession. Unless he had some compelling reason to do his business in a glass-and-steel office building downtown, he just might have come here. Two tellers were on duty, their combined ages probably didn't equal mine. There was no point in asking them what they were doing seven years ago--probably trying to grow breasts. But the customer service rep looked more promising, if age was the only criterion.

"Yes, may I help you, sir?" She was thin, stiff, and dry, with a voice to match. I wondered if she'd ever been as young as the kids in the teller cages. Even though I wasn't asked, I sat down. Her desk was one of those tiny ones that banks issue to lower-level management. The desks have no drawers and the employees get demerits if the top is untidy. I was glad I didn't work for a bank.

"My name is Garrett. I'm an investigator engaged by the family of one of your depositors. He disappeared seven years ago."

My charm had failed to impress her. "Yes, sir."

"The man is Daniel Wilson. A lawyer. He lived not far from here. Our records indicate he used your bank, although I'm not sure if he used your branch."

She gave me the kind of look that most women reserve for small boys trying to look up their dresses. "You understand that information regarding depositors is confidential."

"I have all the information regarding his financial affairs already. The Shreiner Agency is very thorough." Both statements were true, taken separately.

"Then how can we help?" The way she emphasized "we", she made it clear she wasn't interested in helping. At most she was slightly interested in why I was there at all, if I had the records already.

"I'm looking for people who knew Mr. Wilson." I described him and brought out the photograph. She looked at it for a long time, as if she were thinking of buying it but didn't want to be overcharged.

"I knew this gentleman myself. Not too well, but I certainly remember him." Then she stopped. I was going to have to work for it.

"Tell me what you can recall."

"This is a small branch. When he first opened his accounts, I was a teller. I remember him as pleasant and friendly. And it was a bit unusual, at that time, to have an attorney living in the neighborhood."

"His neighbors say he was a nice fellow."

"Very nice. Never made others wait unnecessarily. Considerate of others. Always had his deposit slips made out before he got in line."

Boy, I thought, this was the stuff of hard-hitting investigations. A few more leads like this and I could forget the case completely. "Did he bank alone?"

"Oh, yes. Always."

"Do you recall seeing him around the time it happened?"

"The Friday before his car was found."

"Anything special about that visit?" I tried to sneak a look at my watch. Almost time to go.

"Just that he wanted to go to his box."

"A safe-deposit box?"

"A large one. Most people just get those tiny ones, budget conscious, and then they run out of room and can't store all their important papers. But Mr. Wilson had the right idea; rented the largest size we have, right from the start."

"Oh, yes," I lied. "We knew there was a box, but not how large." I felt a sense of satisfaction in finding something that Shreiner had missed.

She indicated a series of four brass boxes displayed against the wall.

"The one on the right, there; about the size of four shoeboxes together; that's it."

She was being conservative in her estimate; if you cut off Wilson's arms, legs, and head, you could probably hide his torso in the box. What did a young lawyer; single, living on the cheap, need with it?

"Did he use the box often?"

"Every time he made a deposit. He usually took about half his check in cash, and then went to the box."

"Tell me what you remember about that visit."

"He came in just before the late afternoon rush. That was unusual in itself; he ordinarily banked just before we closed on Friday evenings. He cashed his entire check; no deposit and asked to visit his box. He took two briefcases in with him. One was large, like a small suitcase—"

"A transfer case"

"That's the word, thank you. He was in the room with his box a long time. When he left the cases seemed to be heavy."

"Was he alone that time?"

"Oh, yes."

"Did he seem nervous or emotional?"

"Not that I can recall. He certainly wasn't unpleasant, if that's what you're asking."

I asked some more questions, but nothing that led anywhere. I thanked her and left. The case was starting to move; I just couldn't decide in what direction. Enough cash to fill a briefcase and a transfer case was enough to get out of town and not come back. After he got rid of the car, he must have taken some other form of transportation. Using a rental car leaves a paper trail, and Shreiner's report showed no record of a car rental in his name.

Walking away from the stuff in his apartment wasn't a problem. If he was carrying that much cash, he could replace anything he needed. I thought about the logistics of what I understood so far. He drives the car to a country road and sets it up to look like he's dead. How does he get clear? He has a long way to go, somewhere, and he isn't going to be happy about walking around with those cases. He stashes them first, then gets rid of the car, walks as far away as he can, and then hitchhikes and at the end of the ride he gets a cab. Maybe he switches cabs a couple of times to muddy the trail. He gets back to where he stashed the cash. He takes a low visibility form of transportation, busses or trains, where he can pay cash till he gets where he's going. If he left the money at the station, he would be all set.

I didn't know where he'd run, or why he'd run, but no judge was going to believe the coincidence, if the part about the money came out in court. And if that was the way it was, there was nothing I could do. I hated the idea of charging someone to prove the other side's case. It was starting to look like I wasn't going to be a helpful witness for the estate. I consoled myself that at least I'd found something that Shreiner's hadn't. Then it occurred to me that Shreiner's might have known. They'd seen his deposits and his income tax returns and the fact that he paid for a safe deposit box rental. They were just too smart to put it in the report. Maybe, like my ex-wife always told me, I wasn't so smart after all.

That still didn't explain why Shreiner's would drop the case without explanation. Sometimes the investigation goes one way and sometimes another. You are careful what you put to paper, but you don't quit just because a little unfavorable evidence comes up.

I took a bus back to Center City.

The law firm of Wilson, Strasnick & Mendelson occupied half of the fifteenth floor of one of the new high rises near City Hall. Even by the standards of a Center City law office, it was imposing. Real Oriental rugs lay on top of the gray wall-to-wall carpeting, and the waiting room was done up as an Old English reading room, with dark paneling, brass wall sconces, and heavy, comfortable chairs and tables. On the wall across from me the magazine rack offered the current issues of *Forbes, Smithsonian, The New York Review of Books, Connoisseur, and Atlantic Monthly*. I felt out of place, even in my best suit. Fortunately, I was alone in the reception room. I picked up Forbes and pretended to read.

A little after four a blonde receptionist who'd stepped straight from the pages of a fashion magazine, with a side trip to the jewelers, appeared. I wondered who her boyfriend was. Whoever, he was a lucky guy. She ushered me into a conference room with a table big enough to seat twenty. It was simply furnished, but its sheer size, in downtown Philadelphia, spoke of even more money than the reception area. I became conscious of the stain on my tie.

A deeply tanned man in his late thirties entered by another door and offered his hand. He wasn't wearing a suit jacket and he'd loosened his tie. He wore red suspenders. "Strasnick, Mr. Garrett. Pleased to meet you."

Even if he really wasn't at least he seemed to be. His smile expressed itself in more than just his mouth, or even his eyes. It gave a good-natured, wrinkled glow to his whole face. His dark hair; thinning on the sides, was perfectly groomed. So were his nails, I noticed as my eye caught a gold pinky ring with a diamond. He looked strong and fit, and his shirt bulged at the top buttons. There was also some bulging at the bottom buttons. A few too many good meals at Le Bec Fin, I decided. I caught myself trying to pull in my own stomach.

We sat down at one comer of the table. "I appreciate your time on short notice."

"We're busy this time of year. We're still digging out from all the year-end work. I'm in the middle of a settlement right now, but we're waiting for the title company to get a power of attorney up here, so I can give you a few minutes till the documents arrive. But I'm rambling. I'll make time for anything to do with Dan but the more I talk the more I'm wasting your time."

"There's a hearing scheduled for Monday. I'm trying to find out what happened."

"I already gave my deposition to the insurance company. I have nothing to add."

"I'm working for the family."

"Yes, so you said." I gave him Mark Louchs's card. He glanced at it and handed it back.

"As I understand it, the life insurance is related to his partnership interest," I said.

"It funds the buyout of his partnership share--it gives the firm the money to pay a lump-sum settlement with him—or rather, his heirs. If he's declared dead, the money goes to the firm and then to his estate."

"I assume the firm is the beneficiary, then?"

"Technically. We don't benefit; it's a pass-through. Every nickel comes in and goes out. Now, then," he said more briskly. "What questions about Dan can I answer for you?"

"Let's start with how you got together."

He glanced at his watch, just slowly enough to make sure I'd see it. "I'm not sure what that has to do with anything."

I wasn't going to tell him about my discovery of the safe deposit box and what that meant for our prospects, so I phrased it in a more general way. "I need to know everything I can--any little thing that might help convince the judge he's really dead."

"We met in law school. Going into business was my idea. I thought we'd make a good mix. He was sharp and a hard worker, but not a client getter. Too shy. Clients think you're being aloof. I told him, I'll get them in the door; and we'll do the work together."

"What were his outside interests?"

"In law school, none that I knew of. All any of us did, back then, was work. But later, when we were in partnership, he loved to travel. Didn't matter where--driving around the area, trips to Europe, a week in Canada, anything to get out of town."

"What did he do on his trips? Make business contacts? Meet people? Bring back souvenirs?"

"Never mentioned anything but the usual travel stories: how the car broke down, how it rained in London, the food, things like that. He was never secretive about his trips. If you asked him on Monday where he'd been, he'd tell you."

"Did he go alone?"

"As far as I knew. He never mentioned taking anyone."

"Did he have girlfriends?"

"I don't particularly recall if he dated in law school or not. But he had a decent social life as far as I could tell. There was one girl he dated for a year or so; we had them to the house once or twice."

"Can you remember her name?"

"Sorry. It was a long time ago."

I tried not to think about how many times I'd be hearing that in the next three days. "Did he always live alone?"

"That's one thing I know for certain. Never had a roommate. The way he lived, he really had no need. He was a pretty frugal guy except for the travel."

"What kind of work does the firm do?"

"General civil practice, with an emphasis on trial work. Personal injury, Jones Act, workmen's comp, commercial, construction cases, plus some office practice. Like the real estate settlement in the other conference room," he added pointedly.

"What about when he was here?"

"The same. Just not as much of it, and the cases weren't as good."

"What do you know about his disappearance?"

"My impression was, he was burning out. He was coming into the office late, which was unheard of for him, and stopped coming in on weekends at all. He seemed tired. He said he wasn't sleeping well. If I remember it right, he'd broken up with the girl I mentioned. He asked to see a copy of the partnership agreement-- said he wanted to review his options. It made me nervous, of course, but I gave it to him. I wasn't sure how serious he was about leaving. Certainly, he didn't mention a definite decision or a date or anything like that. I would have sat down for a long talk with him if he'd said anything specific. I wanted him to stay. If he'd needed a couple months off to recharge his batteries, we could have worked it out."

"How close in time was this request for the partnership agreement to his disappearance?"

He thought for a moment. "The same week, or the week before. It wasn't long."

"What happens to his share of the partnership since his disappearance?"

"According to our partnership agreement, the only entitlement to a share is upon death or withdrawal. There's nothing to administer for now."

"Can I have a copy?"

"Sorry, its proprietary."

"Certainly. I understand." I knew he'd turn me down; perhaps now he'd give me what I really wanted. "Can you just tell me the amount of life insurance payable?"

"One hundred thousand dollars."

"Did he have any enemies?"

"Oh, there were a couple of lawyers who bore grudges, and a disgruntled client or two, but no one ever made any threats that I was aware of. Certainly no one who would attempt to kill him."

"What do you think happened?"

He leaned back in his away from me, and spread his hands, palms upward. He shook his head "What happened? I don't know. I've thought about this for seven years and I still don't know. He was under a lot of pressure, working way too hard. I think he made some bad decisions."

"Meaning he staged this to cover his tracks and disappear?"

He looked me in the eye. "I think he committed suicide and tried to make it look like a homicide."

"You'd better take this one step at a time."

"That last few months, he was very tense, very unhappy. He had no wife or children. No one to give him any perspective, take his mind off his troubles. This kind of thing sometimes happen. This is a high-pressure job. People blow small problems out of proportion. He was always a worrier. That was part of why he was such a good lawyer; he couldn't shut his mind off. There was always something to think about. As far as why to make it look like a homicide or like an accident, I don't know. Maybe he thought suicide would be a shame to his family. He was very close to them. Some people still feel that way. He was from a Polish Catholic family. I don't know about him personally, but his mom was religious. And besides, the insurance policy pays double for death by accident or homicide, and nothing in case of suicide except a refund of premiums. That doesn't matter to the firm, but it would matter to his beneficiaries. And in case you're wondering, if the policy pays double, that makes no difference to the firm. The extra goes straight to the estate either way." He paused, touching his fingertips together. "I know that's not enough of a reason to kill yourself. We were really hitting our stride. The money was in staying alive, not one insurance check. And no, it doesn't make a lot of sense. But that's all I've got. And I'm sorry but I have to go."

He stood up and extended his hand. The fashion model was at the conference room door to show me out.

CHAPTER THREE
Friday, 5:00 P.M.

I USED A PAY PHONE in the lobby to call the Powell Township Police Department. I had no trouble reaching the chief--he answered the phone himself. The officer who'd done the Wilson investigation was no longer around; he'd moved to Ohio a couple of years before. But the chief said he was familiar with the case and was working that night anyway. He agreed to meet me at seven.

A cold and burnt-orange sun was hanging low to the west when I walked outside Strasnick's office building. Although it was an hour till sunset, the shadows cast by the buildings had already darkened the street. Wind blew through my overcoat as I walked down JFK Boulevard toward my Honda. I'd found a space in an alley off Eighteenth Street behind a dumpster; when I got back, not only was the paint job still intact, but there was no ticket. It was enough to brighten my mood.

I headed west, out of the city. I lived in a down-at-the-heels garden apartment complex in an unfashionable part of the Main Line behind Radnor. My clothes, the furniture, and the Honda were all I had to show for my marriage. Well, not quite; it depends on whether you count my disbarment. My wife had wanted the Audi when we separated, even though we'd bought the Honda for her. It suited me; there was less money owing on the Honda and it was a good car for my work. People will notice, sooner or later, an Audi parked in one place very long. But a white Honda Civic with no window decals and no special antennas can sit for a week without anyone noticing or remembering it afterward. Even though it was just after five, the traffic moved smoothly. Philadelphia's traffic is completely unpredictable. I used to think it was the unsynchronized traffic lights, but it's more than that. There's a perversity about whether the streets are busy or not that defies the law of averages. You can be stuck in what looks like rush hour traffic on the Schuylkill or Roosevelt Avenue at seven in the morning, fight your way through to downtown, and find it deserted. And the next day it takes only ten minutes to get downtown, then half an hour in gridlock to get the last three blocks to your office.

I parked in the main parking lot in front of the complex. Even though I had an assigned space, I never parked there, or even in the same space I'd parked the day before. When I was a lawyer, handling a tough domestic case for the wife, the husband looked up where I lived, slashed the Audi's tires, and pissed on the front seat. You learn from such things, especially when the weather turns warm.

The apartment wasn't dirty; neither was it clean. Mainly it was dusty. During the week I ate my meals out, and I only cooked on weekends if there was no surveillance going on. Since that's what I did almost every Saturday night, the kitchen was hardly used. When I did eat at home, I usually ate off paper plates. I slept there, of course, except for the rare all-night stakeouts and the even rarer nights when a woman invited me home.

I got out of my suit and changed into jeans, insulated boots, a heavy flannel shirt, and a parka. I checked my answering machine and my answering service from the office; no messages of consequence.

Back at the car, I opened the trunk and made sure my equipment was still there. A good quality camera with a tripod and a serious zoom lens. Two flashlights--a tiny pencil beam and an ordinary two-cell one when I felt like blending in. A box of music CDs and a quart bottle with a wide mouth for pissing in, both essential for stakeout work. Bottled water and protein bars. A powerful set of night binoculars. Some people in the business recommended infrared scopes; my experience is that anyone you'll be watching at night is moving around in some sort of light anyway, usually streetlights or headlights, so a good pair of night binoculars is enough. Plus, the scopes are expensive.

The last item was an ordinary toolbox with a couple of wrenches, a socket set, a small hammer, some assorted screwdrivers, and the usual miscellany of picture hangers, screws, and washers. I never used any of the hardware; it was there only as camouflage for my burglar's tools. By themselves, the picks and pry-bars would have stood out. Not that I did many inside investigations, to use the euphemism, but every once in a while . . .

I looked around the parking lot, satisfied myself that no one was watching, and started up. I liked to keep the inside of the car bare, as a precaution against theft and to keep the car from being noticed. All that was in the driver's compartment with me was an empty Thermos behind the passenger seat and a .357 magnum with a four-inch barrel under the driver's seat in a holster. I rarely carried the gun on a job, even though I had a license. For one thing, if you get yourself into a situation where you need a gun, you've made a mistake at the start. Second, Pennsylvania's laws on carrying a handgun are contradictory. A handgun license is statewide in scope; but it is also a misdemeanor to carry a gun within the city limits of Philadelphia--which is the place you need one the most anyway. No one had resolved the conflict, and I didn't feel like being the test case.

I made good time on the turnpike. By the time I reached the rest stop just before the Morgantown exit, I figured I had enough time for a hamburger. I ate with one hand and held open the police information part of the Shreiner file with the other. It wasn't the actual report; under a peculiar Pennsylvania statute relating to police record-keeping, it would have been illegal for the police to allow that to be copied. But clearly the Shreiner people had seen the report, because their summary was extensive.

A telephone call was received at Powell Township via County Radio around 2230 hours Sunday night about a car and a shooting on Route Ten near Mohnton Road. The caller, a female, gave her name as Lisa Wilson. Because it was a shooting, units from the state police and from the adjoining township, Brecknock, were also asked to respond. Sergeant Dietz from Powell Township arrived about ten minutes after the call was received. A Ford Pinto, four years old, was found in a patch of trees in a lane near the intersection. The driver's window and the passenger's window were both shattered, and there were two bullet holes in the front left fender above and to the rear of the wheel. The car was stuck in the mud but otherwise drivable. The keys were missing, and the headlights were off. The transmission was in park. Gas tank was half full. The front interior was covered in blood. Because of "muddy conditions in the area and road traffic on Route Ten, it was impossible to identify any footprints or tire tracks as being associated with the vehicle." I sighed and rubbed my eyes. I knew crap when I saw it. If the area was muddy, it would have held great footprints. The trouble is, if you step all over them with size twelve boots, all you get is size twelve footprints of yourself. I had met a hundred ham-fisted Sergeant Dietzes. I was sure he roamed all over the scene with his piece out, playing hide-and-seek with his own shadow, until the state police arrived, called him a goddam dumb asshole for destroying evidence, and sent him off to direct traffic.

The rest was a summary of the lab reports. The blood was human, type O positive, which narrowed the candidates down to about half the population of North America. The car was registered to Daniel Wilson. All the identifiable prints in the car--which weren't many--were his. Examination of the engine compartment revealed two .45 bullets, both badly flattened by impact with the engine block. At least one of the rounds was a hollow point, for enhanced expansion on impact; the examiner wasn't sure about the other. End of file. Besides, it was time to be going.

I was surprised by the Powell Township Police Station. Most of the township police departments have a little office tacked onto the township sheds. This was a handsome, one-story building with polished brown linoleum floors and bright fluorescent lighting. The dispatcher on duty directed me to the chief. His office was for work, not display. Wanted posters and missing children bulletins were thumbtacked, taped, or nailed to every inch of wall space.

Files, many of them capped with empty coffee cups, were piled everywhere; he had to clear a stack off one of the chairs so I could sit down. The air was thick with cigarette smoke, and I counted three overflowing ashtrays on his desk.

The chief--he introduced himself as Harry Ziemer—was a tall, beefy man, about fifty, his eyes in a permanent squint from too many years of traffic duty in the summer sun. He pumped my band once, hard, and sat down.

"I know this is short notice and that this is an old file, Chief. Thanks for taking the time to meet with me."

"It's still open." I saw the case folder sitting on the middle of his desk.

"I'd like to see it cleared as much as you would."

"It's the only one of these we got." It was a simple statement of fact, but it sounded defensive. I wondered if the township supervisors or the DA was riding him about the case, or if this was purely a matter of professional pride.

I looked at him and then at the file, wondering what was inside. "This thing cause much of a fuss when it happened?"

"Oh, yeah; not the shooting so much---victim wasn't from around here, you know. But the part about not finding the body. Gets all the speculation going. And the big-city TV reporters out here for their story, too." His voice had the pleasant, singsong rhythm of the Pennsylvania Dutch, but his tone wasn't pleasant. "Lots of stupid-ass questions, most of them by fellers I thought were pretty smart. Trying to make this place look like a dumping ground for Philadelphia killings."

"Chief, I'm not out to give anybody any publicity about anything. I work for the survivors of this fellow, trying to help them. His mother and sister. This hearing I told you about on the phone-- well, if the judge thinks that Wilson is dead, then he'll release the life insurance money and anything else that's been tied up all these years. Help the living. I'd just like you to tell me what you've got. Maybe it'll help me, maybe not."

"My department's looked bad enough out of this. And I wasn't even chief back then."

"If I can help clear this case there'll be lots of good publicity. And you're the chief now." It sounded too blatant, so I decided to back off. "The main thing is that it really can't hurt the township; it can only help. And no one needs to testify. I just need to know what you know."

"What I tell you is off the record."

I nodded. He paused for a moment, and then nodded back. He put on his reading glasses and opened the file. I told him what I knew already. He nodded slowly as I spoke, thumbing through the pages. When I finished he put aside most of the file and left a few sheets and a big envelope between us.

"Here's what else we got. The stateys went over the car real careful, now. There was a fourth bullet. It nicked the left post of the windshield at about eye level. Like the others, it was moving perpendicular to the car, left to right. After the nick it kept on going; no bullet recovered. But the lead tracing matched the slugs from the engine. One shell casing was found at the scene, a forty-five. They found hair samples from at least two different people in the car. But that don't mean shit; anybody that gets in your car can leave a hair or two, and they can stay there for months. For what it's worth, one sample was short, dark, and brown; another was long and blond. We matched up the blond sample by microscopic comparison with a former girlfriend, Elizabeth Chatwin; the short brown hair was the victim's. There was no firing inside the car. There were very faint powder markings on the left side of the car and on the outside of the glass fragments from the driver's window. Not concentrated around the bullet strikes; more spread out. It's not in the report, and the criminologist said she wouldn't testify to it in a criminal case, but she thinks it means that the vehicle was moving when the bullets struck. The shots were from too close range to leave any powder residue, but without knowing the speed of the cars and whether the shots came from a moving vehicle, she won't even try to guess on the range. No more than six or seven feet, though."

"What about powder marks on the driver's window?"

He laughed. "Oh, yeah, Dietz was interested in that, too. The fragments from the driver's door went inward; they were mainly inside the car. The ones from the passenger's side went outward, all over the road. He got together all the glass fragments--some off the road and some from the inside of the car--and shipped them off to the FBI crime lab in Washington in two envelopes. Asked them to please reconstruct the window and test it for powder and the angle of the bullet. The package came right back, along with a note telling us we had to be kidding. When I opened it, I saw what they meant. Your car windshield is safety glass; it's got a layer of plastic-like stuff in between two layers of glass so it stays together even when it breaks. But your side windows are tempered glass; they shatter into a million little pieces. No way you'll ever piece them together. All we can tell is, a bullet came in the driver's window, probably went through the occupant, and out the other side."

He put the report to one side and passed me the photographs. I had seen dozens of crime scene photos in the past, state police black-and-white eight-by-ten glossies, and yet being handed a packet of them always made my stomach jump. You could look at two or three perfectly ordinary shots of a damaged car, just like you would see in the morning paper, and the next one would be a decapitated corpse. Or a skeleton trying to get out of a burned-out pickup truck, its bony hand on the door handle that a few hours before had been too hot for him to touch. Or just a photograph of a shoe lying in the road, a long way from the impact, with a foot in it.

These were bloody, of course, but nothing like what I'd seen before. The first one showed the Pinto from the side, most of the detail washed out. The illumination seemed to be from the headlights of a patrol car. The two bullet holes in the fender showed up clear and black as a pair of eyes. The car was nose-down and tilted slightly to the right, I assumed the ground was lower further off the road, under the right wheels.

The next few shots were close-ups of the fender holes, some from the outside and some taken with the hood open. In several of them, someone had passed strings through the holes to the points where the rounds struck the engine, indicating the paths of the bullets. I was surprised; normally they go to this kind of trouble only to document the path of rounds through a human body. The strings indicated that the rounds had come from slightly to the rear. The next shot showed the strings as seen from the front of the car; looking back at their level. The strings were pointing up at an angle, maybe thirty degrees, indicating that the bullets had been fired from slightly above. Then I realized the car was tilted, too; if it was level the strings would be only slightly tilted. So the shooter was a little above the level of where the bullets hit. If the car was level, that is. You could get a headache thinking about reconstruction too much. The main thing was that the strings converged at a point a few feet away from the car, indicating that all the rounds had been fired from approximately the same place relative to the Pinto. That meant the shooter was moving at roughly the same speed as the Pinto, and that the shooter squeezed off all four rounds very quickly, at night, from a moving car, shooting at another moving car. It didn't seem likely that the shooter had also been the other driver. That put two men in the shooter's car, and that one of them was experienced. Before I learned the details of the shooting I wondered why Wilson had pulled his cash out of the bank.

Now I was wondering who else could have known about it. There were several interior shots of the car; the lighting was good, probably with some kind of bounce flash. Blood was splattered and smeared everywhere around the front seat, more on the driver's side than the passenger's. There was blood spatter on the underside of the roof. I handed them back. "Any neutral witness statements?"

"No. This is a rural spot. Nearest house is a half mile away, and it's mostly forested. Blankets the noise. People might not have heard anything at a quarter of a mile. We talked to the nearest residents anyway; nobody could add a thing."

"What about Lisa Wilson's statement?"

His eyebrows knitted. "Isn't she your client?"

"Yes and no. I represent the estate. If the victim left no will it all goes to his mom. If he left a will then the sister might stand to benefit, if he put her in. I don't know. But either way, I haven't talked to her yet. That's for tomorrow morning. I'd like to know what she said that evening."

The chief looked uncomfortable. Like most policemen-- or lawyers, for that matter--he had great faith in the first version witnesses tell, no matter how fragmentary or confused, before they have time to think about what story would suit their interests best. He picked up a two-page typewritten report with a signature at the bottom.

"I'm not going to read all the crap. The investigating officer wasted a lot of time here. Even gave her the Miranda warnings, God knows why. Dumbass move. Anyway, here we go. Statement was taken at the station here starting at about twenty-three-thirty hours. Witness had arrived at the station at twenty-three-hundred hours and had to wait for Dietz to return from the scene of the investigation. Witness says she had been shopping. She was in Philadelphia for a visit from her home in Los Angeles. The victim and the witness were in separate cars. He had his own Pinto; she was driving a car registered to her mother. Witness produced her mother's registration and proof of insurance. She said that the two of them were supposed to meet at a gas station in Morgantown and she was to follow him to Green Hills, a restaurant up Route Ten. He knew the road and where the restaurant was, and she didn't. He didn't show up; she waited. She tried to call his office, his home, her mother, trying to find where he was. Finally, she started up Route Ten northbound, going towards the restaurant. She thought she may have misunderstood about where to meet. And it was the only other place she could think of where he could possibly be. She found the car; no one around, no body. She had seen a couple of sets of southbound headlights as she approached the scene but thought nothing of it till she saw the car. Then she called nine-one-one, who put her in touch with our township. She drove to the station on her own after making her call. Very upset. Said victim had been in good spirits, didn't see him very often since her move to California, had no reason to think he was in danger. No leads re enemies. Victim was lawyer in Philadelphia, unsure if handled drug or organized crime cases. There's more, about his address and stuff like that." He put the report back in the file and shut it with finality. I had questions, but I had the sense the chief had more to say.

"Mr. Garrett, a couple of things I didn't mention. We didn't put them in the report because they might have given a defense lawyer ammunition if we ever filed charges. Dietz was suspicious of her. No particular reason. She seemed like a nice girl who'd just seen something terrible, and she was really upset. She wasn't a real suspect, but she was all we had. He checked the back seat of her car. With her consent, of course. It was full of shopping bags. Dated receipts showing she'd been shopping that day. Women's clothes and shoes, mostly. She'd shopped in the Reading outlet malls in the morning and at Park City over in Lancaster in the afternoon. And we checked her for powder; just a real basic rub-down test. The test gives a lot of false positives, but not this one. Negative. She hadn't fired a gun or been near anyone firing a gun."

"You didn't let anything pass."

"With no witnesses, a car that looks like it's been shot from close range? What would you think?"

"What about the restaurant?"

"Green Hills is up the road a few miles. We checked, there was a reservation for two for eight o'clock for Wilson. No one showed up. Hostess remembered it 'cause they were so busy that night that they held the table forty minutes and then gave it to somebody else. She was afraid they'd show up a little late and be mad. Reservation had been made by Daniel Wilson several days before. The hostess remembered he was polite and well-spoken. And that the connection wasn't the greatest, like he might be calling from Philly, so it all fits."

"Is that it?"

"That's what we've got, unless you want to look at the ballistics. That's from the state crime lab but it's not going to tell you anything. All recovered rounds were from the same .45, which doesn't do much good since no gun was recovered."

"One more question, Chief. Well, two if you count giving me some directions. What do you think?"

He shrugged his shoulders. "There was talk, rumors, that it might be organized crime. You hear talk all the time. Especially about doings over there." He jerked his head in the direction of Reading. "But we could never pin anything down. Mainly, it didn't quite look like a mob killing. The shooter was a pro of some kind, but the rest of it was fishy. Those guys either leave the body at the scene; or if they kidnap him, the victim just disappears, and no one suspects there was a crime. Pretty half-baked stuff, this, if it was organized crime. So, there was no obvious motive and the MO was wrong."

"The sister?"

He shook his head decisively. "Didn't see her that night, but I met her on a re-interview a week or so later when Dietz was unavailable. She wouldn't hurt a fly. Really sweet girl. Wish my own daughter was half that nice. The powder test proved she didn't fire a gun. Plus, if she had done it, she was smart enough to come up with a better story."

"So then what?"

"Random killing. Some guy on drugs, or crazy, driving by, not from around here, picks out Mr. Wilson. Maybe he thought Wilson cut him off or something and it was a road rage thing. Drives past, or hides by the side of the road, pulls out a forty-five. Could have been back in New Jersey or Maryland within an hour." He said it as if being from New Jersey or Maryland was enough motivation for being a random killer.

"What about the body?"

"This is pretty rough country. Not so good for farming, not like down in Lancaster. Could have put it in an old well or a mine shaft. Used to be mining around here, but no more. Or dumped it in a quarry--couple of abandoned ones around here, flooded up. Even might stick it in a ravine if he didn't mind the chance that some hunter would find it. Or took it with him. Who can say about crazy people?"

"There's no telling what crazy people will do." Or sane ones, for that matter, if they're pressed hard enough. It seemed as good as Strasnick's theory. Or any I had, for that matter. I took directions, thanked him, and headed out. It was fortunate that Route Ten ran in front of the station, so all I had to do was follow it. In the next seven miles I saw less than a dozen signs of human habitation, and no streetlights or signs at all. The only other traffic was a single set of headlights behind me. The road rose, fell, and twisted as if it were trying to throw me. Once I failed to appreciate how quickly a turn was coming up, braked hard, and skidded right up to a stone wall. From the paint smears on the stone, others hadn't been so lucky. Large trees, mostly pines, lined both sides of the road and seemed to meet overhead.

He had said I'd be in Morgantown a half mile beyond the spot if I missed it, and sure enough, the road curved to the left one last time, straightened, and brought me right up to the turnpike toll booths. I turned around, watched my odometer carefully, and found the spot on the second try. I drove by slowly a couple of times each way and then got out.

Even by Route Ten standards, it was a desolate place. It was not even a real intersection; the road branching off was simply a muddy path, graveled in spots, heading generally toward the east. Coming from the south, the main road was in the middle of a long left-hand curve where it intersected the path. Looking further north, the road went over a crest and out of sight about a hundred yards away. Heavy pines on both sides. To the east of the curve the land was flat, but to the west across the road, it sloped upward to a bank about twenty feet high. About half the area was covered with a thin coat of snow; the rest was either bare or ice puddles.
The intersection itself was broad and flat enough for several cars to park; it must be a popular place during deer season, I thought. I stood about where I figured the Pinto had been; big trees to the north and south obscured the view from both directions. It was easy to see it as you passed by, but not till you got close.

I opened my trunk and took out a hundred-yard steel tape and my big flashlight. I was about to turn on the light when the three-quarter moon came out between two clouds. The additional light wasn't much, but it was enough for something shiny to catch my peripheral vision. My night vision wasn't what it had been in

Vietnam, but there it had been good enough to save my life, and peripheral vision was where night vision is best anyway. I had seen something shiny. Woods weren't supposed to have shiny things. Or cars full of blood and bullet holes, for that matter.

Without turning my head, I looked to my left. Up on the bank, about thirty to forty yards from me, was the upper part of a car; not the grill or hood, just the windshield. It was facing me, parked back from the edge of the bank. No lights. Somebody had gone to the trouble to find the spot but not pull up to the edge. Somebody wanted to watch this spot, this night, and didn't want to be seen. No cars had passed me in either direction since I'd stopped. A car had been behind me when I left the police station. I struggled to recall; no, it hadn't been behind me when I turned around at Morgantown. There was no good reason for that car to be up there, if it was the same one. Well, not for sure; maybe a couple of teenagers looking for a place to park happened to follow me. And maybe not.

I reached into the trunk once more, pulled out a piece of twine and a small grease pencil, replaced the big light with my pencil light, and slammed the lid as hard as I could. The sound echoed for a moment, bouncing back once before being absorbed by the trees. I thought about how the four shots that night must have sounded. Then, as casually as I could, I opened the driver's door and leaned in. Using my body to block the view, I reached under the seat and snatched up my .357 magnum. On the off chance they had a Starlite scope or infrared, I jammed it into a pocket of the parka before turning around. Turning on the flashlight, I made a show of measuring the distance between the road and the closest tree, then the width of the path where the trees ended. I held up a little notebook and a pencil but didn't bother to write anything down. There was no activity from the car. I walked down the path about ten yards, moving the flashlight from side to side as if I was looking for something, seven years later, that the police had missed. Stepping behind a tree, I looked back, the car was barely visible through the network of branches. I found a small rock for a weight and tied it and the flashlight to the end of a branch. It hung down to waist level and swung convincingly back and forth in the light breeze. I looked at my watch, I figured I had ten minutes, maybe fifteen, before they would become suspicious.

My first instinct was to drop to my hands and knees, or at least a crouch, but that might have made me visible underneath the canopy of pine branches. So I just moved slowly from tree to tree, avoiding the middle of the path, until I was another twenty yards down the trail. Just ahead, I could see where it ended in a clearing full of wrecked cars and rusted washing machines. Someone's dream of a cabin in the woods that never came off.

When I was sure I was out of sight, I headed north through the trees, moving as quickly as I could in the dark. And working my way back to the road under cover. The ground was flat, and moonlight reflected off the dusting of snow. I didn't care how much noise I made if I couldn't be seen. When I estimated I'd gone far enough, I cut to the left. Moving more and more carefully as I approached the road, I dropped to my knees and then to my belly. The car wasn't visible; unless it had moved, it was out of sight to my left around the curve of the bank. I crawled out to the very edge of the road. Still nothing. Moving as slowly as I dared, I inched out onto the road. I felt safer; the pavement was warmer than the snow and would provide less contrast for an infrared scanner. Plus, my parka would blend into the black pavement. The bank across the road was steep, but thick with grasses, weeds, and branches. It was an easy climb. I reached the top, waited for the moon to pass into another cloud, and stuck my head slowly up over the rim.

At some point, years ago, the area on the west side of Ten had been bulldozed and cleared, probably to make room for a couple of houses. It was flat as far as I could see, at least a hundred yards, and there was a view of Morgantown and a valley. I could even see a glimpse of the turnpike. I looked away quickly to preserve my night vision. The car was about thirty yards away, directly across the road from my car, facing towards it. The engine was running but no lights were on. No one appeared to be outside.

I pulled out the gun and eased myself up the bank and onto the flat. Lying prone, I counted off sixty seconds. The snow began to seep through the cuffs in my parka and the gaps between the buttons. There was no movement from the car. Very slowly, I got up into a low crouch and circled around to the rear. If they were watching for me down at the site of the shooting they would likely be paying no attention behind. If it was a couple of kids, it didn't matter anyway.

I worked my way around to the rear of the car, keeping a good distance away, and checking around for backup. There was none. I avoided staying directly behind the car. There was always the chance that the moon would come out when the driver decided to check his rearview mirror. Instead, I got down on my stomach and crawled up until I was nearly at the right rear wheel. Again, I counted to sixty. I kept the gun trained on the passenger's door.

I checked the moon; it was behind a large cloud. No danger of an inopportune appearance for at least a couple of minutes. Very slowly I got up on one knee. I kept the gun at knee level; no point in presenting any metal surfaces to catch light.

The instrument lights were on. Two men were in the front seat. The driver was wearing a hat. The passenger was looking down in the direction of my car with a viewing scope. There was no way to tell what it was except that a power cord ran from it to the dash. The driver was holding a telephone to his ear. I looked at the roof: cellular phone and CB antennas, plus a third antenna I didn't recognize.

I got back down and moved away a few yards. The car was a new Ford Taurus, four-door either white or beige. The license plate frame was from a Philadelphia dealership. Using the grease pencil, I took down the number on my forearm. Then I carefully backed away and retraced my path across the road. I waited again for a minute before approaching the flashlight I'd left tied to the tree. When I was satisfied I was still alone, I put my gun back in my parka, retrieved the flashlight and went back to my car. I would have felt better checking the engine for signs of a bomb, but there was no way to do that inconspicuously. It wasn't much comfort to think that if they wanted me dead they could have picked me off from across the road.

The engine started fine, and I thought about my next move. Driving back to the police station would bring them along; but then what? The chief would have them stopped and get their IDs. They would turn out to be two fellows from South Philadelphia who would claim they were checking out prospects for real estate development. And the hell of it was, in addition to shadowing me, it might be true. Any firearms in the car would be registered and licensed. The bills of sale were probably in the trunk. There was nothing to be done. I turned left and headed south to the turnpike; keeping a careful distance, they followed. At the Valley Forge exit I lost them by running the tollbooth. I didn't expect to sleep much that night, but I went home anyway. There was nowhere else to go.

CHAPTER FOUR
Saturday, 7:00 A.M.

I AWOKE AT THREE, tried to get back to sleep till four, and gave up. I didn't know who was in the car, but it was a safe bet that they were the reason the Shreiner Agency was off the case. The fact that they were doing nothing more than watching was no consolation; if they were who I thought they were, there would be no warning if they decided to take me out. I had one foot in the grave already and I didn't even know why.

I took a long shower. If organized crime was simply watching, they wanted something, and that could only be information. It had to be about the Wilson case: I'd never been involved in any other case that could possibly interest them. The fact that they were watching me was a bit of progress in the case, in a way; at least it made hash of the chief's random killer theory. I wish I could say that made me feel better.

I put on a pot of coffee and shaved, looking at my reflection as if it would help. Maybe it wasn't progress after all. Was the chief's theory so impossible? Suppose the organization was interested in Wilson, not necessarily with murder in mind, and then he happened to get killed by a random third party. It could happen, and I needed to make some stretches to make the odd pieces of this thing fit together. With no body, they'd never believe he was dead. They'd assume it was staged to cover his disappearance. They were not people who worked on trust.

What if there were two competing organizations; group A got him; group B was now trying to find out what happened. It wasn't theoretical. I stayed as far away from the mob as I could in my work, but anyone who could read a newspaper knew that the New York mob was trying to take over crime operations in Philadelphia. So who was tailing me? People trying to get information from me or people trying to keep me from getting any? And what about the disappearing money? Had Wilson suspected someone was after him? The fact that he had suddenly pulled out his cash didn't mean he knew he was being targeted. The police records had no mention of finding the cash or empty briefcases. Did someone know about them? If it was murder with robbery as a motive, why hide the body? Maybe someone knew he had the money, but when they stopped him, it wasn't on him. That made sense; if I were him, I would hide the money first and not drive around with it in a car I was going to dump. They might have worked him over at the scene or shot him while stopping him. That would explain the blood in the car. And if he wouldn't talk, they took him somewhere to squeeze the location out of him. So no body. Maybe. It wasn't impossible. Nothing was.

I scrambled a four-egg omelet and put on some bacon. When I'd been married I worried a lot about cholesterol; I didn't care much anymore.

Were the people in the car from the same group that warned off the Shreiner Agency, or a different group? I wasn't sure which was more dangerous. The group trying to obstruct things might leave me alone unless I got close to something big; the others might put the squeeze on me regardless. And after they had what I knew--or rather, when they found out I really knew nothing--my life expectancy could be very short. I had nothing to trade.

I put the food down in front of the window and ate. It was about five-thirty and the sky was beginning to lighten. I had a bad feeling that before the case was over, maybe even before this day was over, there would be trouble; but for now, the coffee was hot, and the eggs tasted good. I ate slowly, taking in the early-morning light and the silence of the streets.

I thought about walking away from it, of course, following in the footsteps of the Shreiner Agency. If it was a matter of my personal safety, I didn't care all that much about Dan Wilson and whether he would get away with it—if he was getting away. I was no hero. I even reached for Louchs's card once; then I thought through what kind of conversation it would be. Mark, I'm getting out. Oh, he would say, quitting on me at the last moment, huh? No, it's just that it's getting too dangerous. So that makes you as gutless as the Shreiner Agency and stupid, too; you knew what you were getting into at the start.

Louchs wouldn't say anything like that, of course, but he'd be thinking it, and so would I. It reminded me of my days, long ago, with the Marines. My squad searched tunnels, rushed tree lines, called in artillery nearly on top of ourselves, jumped feet first into bunkers, and none of us thought of ourselves as brave. We did it because we were afraid to let the others know how scared we were.

Maybe it was a random killing after all, and the boys in the car were interested in me for some other reason? I shook my head; I was back where I started. The more I learned, the less certain I was that there had been a killing at all. The evidence of death was minimal. Anyone serious about disappearing, especially fearing the mob was after him, could go to the trouble of staging what the police had found. The money angle fit. Wilson hadn't gone to the bank on a lark. He'd been there with good reason, and he hadn't intended to come back. But even the bank proved nothing about what happened on Route Ten. Maybe he was trying to disappear when they caught up with him.

Although I'd never had any dealings directly with organized crime, I had a contact. He was expensive, but sometimes for the right price he could come up with inside information. He knew nothing himself; he was more of an information broker. A call to him meant a wait of hours or even days while he checked his own sources. I decided to call him later that morning. Right now, it was time to get ready to meet with Wilson's sister.

I dressed in corduroy slacks, a tweed jacket, and a tie. The sister was a nurse, used to dealing with professionals, and she would expect a tie. As I put on my jacket, I thought about carrying my backup gun, a little .380 automatic. I decided against it; if the pros wanted me dead I'd never see it coming anyway. They didn't get to be pros by shooting it out face-to-face at thirty paces on the main street at high noon. An ice pick in the back of the head, preferably with an unconscious victim, was more their style. I put on my overcoat and headed into the weather.

When I stepped outside I was glad I'd taken my heavy coat. I popped the hood and checked; no tampering that I could see. As additional insurance, I tore a thin strip of paper out of a road map and placed it so that it was caught between the hood and the body when the hood was down. If it disappeared the next time I checked, I'd know the hood had been opened.

I wasn't proud of my office building, but there was no other place to meet a client. I was one of five tenants in an old house in west Philly; we shared an inadequate parking lot and a receptionist/secretary who was worse. It was the kind of place you kept an eye on your hat and coat even in your own office. The other tenants were a decertified CPA who worked as a tax preparer, a passport photograph operation, a real estate broker specializing in apartment rentals to deadbeats, and a "credit counseling" agency. The last two shared most of the same clientele, or at least it seemed that way. The fifth tenant always paid his rent and assessments on time but was never there. I once asked him his business; he smiled and said something about venture capital. I didn't ask again.

I was nearly half an hour early; I'd wanted a few minutes to collect my thoughts and review the Shreiner file again. But as soon as I locked my car door I heard another car door close right behind mine.

I turned and saw a woman in a red down jacket, jeans, and hiking boots. "Hi, you must be Mr. Garrett. I'm Lisa Wilson."

It was a low, pleasant, no-nonsense voice, a little nervous. I looked into dark brown eyes, framed by thick chestnut hair that was tied in a heavy braid that hung to one side. Lisa had a thin, serious face with high cheekbones. There was just a hint of something around her eyes, something faintly exotic, and I recalled that the family was Polish. Just a whisper of the East somewhere in their genes. Her mouth was set in a tentative smile and her hand was extended; I shook it. "Nice to meet you, Miss Wilson."

I unlocked the three bolts that kept the main entrance reasonably secure and motioned her inside. "Go to the top of the stairs and I'll be right with you."

She hung her jacket on the coat rack just inside the door--it would be safe enough on a Saturday with the building locked--and headed up the stairs. She was wearing a clinging white turtleneck, and I stopped to admire the view. She had a nice figure, a narrow waist, and a tight, muscular ass that swayed under her jeans. There was a rawboned, athletic, outdoors look about her that I liked. She took the stairs ahead of me with a loose, bouncy stride while I watched from behind. I'd never laid a hand on a client, either as an attorney or as a private investigator and I wasn't going to start now; but she helped my spirits. Watching her ass was a hell of a lot more interesting than crawling around in the snow trying to keep one step ahead of the men in the car.

I unlocked the door to my office and ushered her inside. Even though she was casually dressed, I was never more aware of the shabbiness of where I did my business: worn carpeting, a scarred desk, and a water-stained ceiling. I hung up my own coat behind the door--I never left my own downstairs, from force of habit.

"Thank you for taking such an interest in my brother's case. I don't think that the other agency would be up this early on a weekend.

"Time is short."

"You want to know what I know about Danny's death."

"Do you think he's dead?"

"Don't you?"

"I don't have an opinion yet. And even if I did, what I think doesn't matter. We need to convince a judge."

She crossed her legs and wound her fingers together around one knee. She looked down at her hands and her voice dropped. "Mr. Garrett, there's something I need to ask before we go any further."

I knew what was probably coming. Thanks a lot, Mark.

"Sure," I said, not meaning it at all.

"Our attorney said that you were very good." I waited for the rest. "He also said that you had been a lawyer yourself."

"As far as how good I am, I'll leave that to your judgment. And yes, I used to practice."

She blushed and looked down at her hands. "I'm really sorry; I hardly know you. But if I'm going to--could you please tell me why you're not a lawyer anymore? This is out of line, but Mr. Louchs said the Shreiner Agency would be good, and then they dumped us at the last minute. Then he told me he'd just hired you. He said that you were really on the ball--that you used to be an attorney. I asked him. He said I should ask you." She paused. "I hope you're not offended."

So Louchs had set it up and left it to me. It was his way of getting back at me for playing with him about taking the case. We were even. I would have to think of a way to get back at him later. I didn't like just being even with a guy like Louchs.

"I was disbarred for dishonesty." The room was very quiet. I could hear the morning traffic picking up outside.

She was still looking at her hands.

"I got out of law school fifteen years ago. I got married right after graduation, my wife was a social worker then. After we'd been married a few years she decided to try law school When she finished, she took the bar and failed. Six months later she failed again, and the next time. She flunked it seven times in all. She was very bright; it was a test anxiety problem. And it got worse with each attempt. She wouldn't sleep for days, couldn't hold anything down, had anxiety attacks. She was seeing a psychiatrist. After the seventh failure she had to be hospitalized for a few days. Too many sleeping pills. They got the pills out of her system and treated her for depression. When she got out she asked me to take it for her, I said no. It was months before the next test date came around and she pleaded with me. I finally said I would. You should have seen how happy she was. Back in those days there was no photo ID; you just showed up, gave them the name, and they handed you the test. Her name was Terri, so no one thought anything about it. I passed it for her, but they were keeping an eye on repeaters. They caught us and disbarred both of us."

"Oh."

"I exhausted my appeals and had to turn in my license, withdraw from my firm. She left. Couldn't stand the guilt."

"I'm sorry. I didn't mean to—"

"It was my decision and I knew the risks."

"You're a very strong person, Mr. Garrett. I'm very grateful you're taking our case."

"Strong isn't the word a lot of people would use."

"Well, I would."

I picked up my pencil. "Were you and your brother close?"

"As close as you can be living across country, at least. I came home once a year and spent time with him and Mom."

"When did you move away?"

She took a moment to think. I noticed that she squinted when she concentrated. "I did two years of community college here, then I moved to Los Angeles for an R. N. program. That would have been, let's see, fourteen years ago this September."

"The last time you saw him, how did he seem?"

"Have you talked to anyone who knew him?" she asked.

"His law partner and a neighbor."

She looked out the window, thinking about what to say. Even though her braid hid part of the side of her face, in profile she was beautiful. She looked back at me. "What did they tell you?"

"He was solitary."

She gave a sad smile. "You're being polite."

"I try not to draw conclusions about people I never met."

"People are solitary when they don't like themselves. He was never a happy person, Mr. Garrett. He liked his work because it was all he had. That last time, he . . . was the same as always."

"What was he depressed about?"

She gave me a sharp look. "People don't decide to get depressed any more than they decide to get happy. But he wasn't depressed. He was just unhappy."

"You need to help me here."

"Growing up was hard for both of us, but he had it worse. Our dad died when he was six. Dad was sick a long time and he didn't have it in him to be much of a father. I had Mom; Dan didn't really have anyone. Mom had to work two jobs, and even as a little kid I was busy helping run the house; there was no time for him to be a kid, have his own friends. He spent his childhood tagging along with me and helping when he could. I loved him, but I was just a sister, not a mom and a dad."

"That made him unhappy thirty years later?"

It was a direct question, maybe a little snide, but she took a long time answering. "There's things you can decide to change about yourself and things you can't. By the time he was grown up, when he disappeared, most of his friends were married, with children. He hadn't found anyone. He just didn't feel he fit in."

"Do you think he could have faked his death and disappeared?"

"I don't think so. I like to think we were close enough that he would have told me if he had been thinking about it. . ."

"You trailed off there."

"I'm sorry. I was just thinking, if it ever occurred to him that disappearing could solve his problems."

"Running away never does."

She looked thoughtful and her fingers toyed with the end of her braid. I wanted to know what she was thinking but there was a job and time was short. "Tell me what happened."

"Well, like I told the Shreiner investigator, I'd been shopping, first at the outlets in Reading and then over near Lancaster at the big mall. Things are so much cheaper here than in Los Angeles. We had agreed to meet for dinner; he said he knew a great French country restaurant with nice atmosphere. He said it was in an old stone house, not like the drywall and paint I was used to seeing in LA. He said it was hard to find, so we were supposed to meet where Route Ten and the turnpike meet near Morgantown. I don't know if we were going to leave my car or I was going to follow him up; we never got that far. I waited for an hour or so. I wasn't worried at first, he was very busy, and something could have delayed him at work, even on a Saturday. It had happened before. He was conscientious about his clients and about getting his work done. I sat in the car and read a paperback book. But after a while, I started to worry. I called his cell and mom at home, but he didn't answer his phone and she didn't know anything. I knew the restaurant was somewhere north on Ten, so I headed that way. If I missed it, I could always get directions at a gas station or a convenience store. Then I saw the car, way off to the side of the road, in the trees."

"What did you do?"

"I got out and yelled for him and looked around as much as I could, till I was sure he wasn't anywhere around. Then I called the police. After that I called my mom, then I went to the police station and gave my statement. I can't remember the name of the police department, but I'm sure you have that somewhere."

"See any footprints or drag marks or anything like that?"

"All I knew was that I couldn't find him." She softened her voice. "And I didn't even have a flashlight; all I could see is what my headlights showed. I didn't see anything about what happened to him."

"Did you go back to LA afterwards?"

"Just long enough to give my notice and pack up. My mom took it very badly--she was sure right from the start that Dan was dead. And with Dad gone, there was no one. It was time to be closer to home."

"Where are you working now?"

"For a small tool and die company. Up near Pottsville. I'm the office manager."

"Not nursing?"

"Ten years as a scrub nurse is enough. And now all this HIV. I was ready for a career change anyway."

I glanced at the clock behind her and saw that it was after eight. It was late enough to call my source. I gave Lisa a missing persons questionnaire to fill out and sent her downstairs. The phone rang at least ten times before he picked up. He said nothing.

"This is Garrett."

"Haven't heard from you in a while." He didn't sound glad to be hearing from me now.

"I haven't taken my business anywhere else, if that's what you're worried about. But I've got some questions."

"You understan', I gotta set the price."

It was the same runaround every time. "First you deliver," I said, putting a hint of weariness into my voice to remind them we haggled every time. "I don't pay to find out who's president."

We had argued enough times that he knew he wasn't going to get anywhere. No matter how badly I needed his help, giving him a blank check was bad for business. "What do you need to know?" It was a nice touch, working "need" into the question. He liked keeping me on edge.

"A lawyer named Daniel Wilson disappeared seven years ago. He was partners with Leo Strasnick, here in town. The way Wilson disappeared it could have been a hit. But there's no body."

He was smarter than he was willing to show. He never asked me to repeat myself, never asked for spelling of a name, and as far as I could tell, never took notes. "You want me to find out if there was a hit? Out of my league. Guys askin' questions like that don't live long."

"I don't need any details. Just find out if Wilson, or Strasnick, was tied to anything. Or in any trouble. That'll be enough."

"Ain't gonna be easy."

"I don't need affidavits. It will be enough if you can find out if either one of them is a familiar name with the guys you know."

It was a left-handed way of bargaining; our words were about the information, but the subtext was how much I was prepared to pay.

"Call me Tuesday noon."

"I need to know by tomorrow."

"Tomorrow? Baby don't bust my chops!"

"No bullshit." I wasn't going to tell him I was under time pressure. That would only drive up the price.

He sighed. "Check back tomorrow afternoon, late. Let it ring twice and then call back." He hung up.

I retrieved Lisa from downstairs and reviewed the questionnaire she had filled out. I didn't learn anything new, but I liked working with my own information and not some other investigator's report. I had to decide for myself what was important--even if I wasn't making much progress.

"How were the police?"

"I know there are families with a disappearance who think the police could have done more, but I don't think so. They gave it a lot of attention, even if they didn't have a lot of resources. They checked into everything."

"Including you."

"It surprised me, but I understood. They had no reason to take my story on faith."

"Where can you be reached?"

"My home address and phone are on the form, but I'm not sure if I'm going home or not before the hearing. If I'm not there I'll be with my mom. It's on there, too."

"Will you be at your mom's the rest of the day today?"

"I have a couple of errands this morning; then I'll be there."

"Would it be convenient to interview your mom around five o'clock? It might go better if you were there."

Lisa looked uncomfortable. "I don't think you'll find she's much help. She doesn't know anything I haven't told you."

"Most of what I do isn't finding things out; it's eliminating certain possibilities."

She looked uncomfortable. "I have to warn you, she can be difficult."

"All the more reason for you to be there."

There was an instant when I thought she was going to argue with me, but it passed. "I'll make sure we're home."

"Say that it won't take long. Thanks again for your help."

She took the hint and collected her things. When I'd finished locking up again and walking her to her car--not a mere courtesy in that neighborhood--she shook my hand again. Not that it mattered, but she wasn't wearing a ring.

Her car had just pulled out into the stream of morning traffic when I saw a man in his late twenties walking slowly toward me. There weren't many people on the street at this hour, and the ones that were out were in no hurry to get anywhere. But he was moving purposefully, and he was looking at me. I could see a glove on the hand I could see; the other was in his pocket. If he had gloves on his hands, there was no good reason to have one in a pocket.

I turned around; another man, a bit older was walking toward me from the other direction. Both his hands were in his pockets and his eyes shifted back and forth from me to the first man. And just behind him was a cream Ford Taurus with multiple antennas on the roof.

Backing up until my back was against my building, I put my own hands in the pockets of my overcoat and found a pocket comb. I inched it forward between my forefinger and index finger until it created a bulge in my pocket. And then I waited.

The older man came within five feet and stopped; the other stayed about ten feet away, to one side, backing him up. They were pros. There was no way I could have had a shot at both, and the older man wasn't blocking the shot of the man behind.

"Come with us, bud "said the older one.

"I don't think so."

"Nobody asked you."

"Oh?"

"You can go in one piece, or a couple."

"Where are we going?"

"Just get in."

"I asked you a question."

"If we wanted you out, you'd be out already." That was my own reasoning, too.

"I'm not moving till you tell me what this is about."

He set his jaw and did the calculation of how much trouble it would be to do something on the street. "There's somebody who wants to talk to you."

"That's what it's about?"

"That's it. Now let's go."

I looked from one to the other and considered my options. "Lead the way."

We got into the Ford, with the younger man driving, the older man in the left-hand back seat, and me in the right back seat. As we drove, the older man frisked me, briefly but thoroughly. He hesitated when he found the comb and looked me in the eye. His look seemed to say that if he was the kind of man who smiled, this would have been worth smiling about. But he wasn't and he didn't. Then be took out a black box with an antenna; it looked like a small walkie-talkie, but I knew it was an FM receiver. He turned it on, sliding through the bands slowly, waiting for a sign that I was carrying a concealed transmitter. A gun they understood; they probably thought it was as normal as carrying a comb. But a wire was different. If the radio went off, the ride wasn't going to end well for me. I was very thankful that the little box didn't make a sound. We made some turns, got onto Lancaster Avenue, and headed east in light traffic. We crossed over the Schuylkill on Vine, made a right at Sixteenth, and parked in front of a small office building near Pine. It took about fifteen minutes and not a word was spoken.

They escorted me to the front door. It was locked, and while they were working the lock I thought about making a run for it. I just might make it around the corner. And then what? They knew who I was, where I worked, probably where I lived, and that I was working on the Wilson case. Running would only buy a little time, and next time they might not be so polite. The younger one took me up to the third floor and directed me to a blank door at the end of the hall. The older one stayed downstairs, presumably watching the stairwell and the fire escape.

The door opened into an office, bare except for a metal desk and two chairs. Some phones, boxes, and coils of cable took up one comer; the room was clearly not in regular use. A slender man in his late fifties was sitting behind the desk. When I came in he was looking down, puzzling over some documents on legal-size paper. After a moment, he put the papers in a drawer and looked up. His hair was mostly gray and cropped very close. Even sitting down, he had a military bearing. He had the look of a man who gave and took orders without discussion. But whatever kinds of orders he dealt in, they were important ones; his suit looked like it hadn't left the store for less than a grand. Strasnick was starting to look ordinary by comparison.

"Mr. Garrett, so glad you could come."

His handshake, like his voice, was hard, powerful, and dry. I was relieved when he let go, as if I'd gotten free of a live electric wire. "Please sit down."

I didn't like that our first interaction was following one of his orders, but there was no point in refusing.

"Let me apologize for the unfortunate events of this morning. I trust you appreciate that it couldn't be helped under the circumstances. As you well know, we are both working under time pressure. Sometimes normal courtesies must be dispensed with. Yes. I'm sure you understand. Now allow me to play host. Would you care for some coffee?"

"Okay." I didn't trust my voice with anything more.

"How do you take it?"

"Black."

He pressed a tiny button on the side of the desk and leaned slightly toward it. "Joseph, two coffees, one black."

"Did you like New York?"

He simply raised his eyebrows, questioning. "That's the way you order coffee there. It comes with cream unless you say black."

He smiled, the way a skull smiles. "Very observant, Mr. Garrett. I found the city very enjoyable." A man I hadn't seen before entered through a side door carrying two Styrofoam cups. He was broad in the shoulders and his hands were thick and powerful. His suit jacket was off, and he was wearing a shoulder holster with a 9mm Beretta, one of the new double-action automatics with a magazine capacity of fourteen rounds. And under his other armpit he carried two spare magazines. His right trouser leg didn't hang smoothly; I figured he had a second gun stashed in an ankle holster. Joseph was not a man to mess with unless you had an infantry platoon backing you up, and he was taking orders from the man in front of me.

Joseph withdrew; neither of us touched our cups. The point of it wasn't to see if I was stupid enough to drink; it was to remove any doubt about who I was dealing with. "Mr. Garrett, like yourself I am an attorney. I am house counsel for various . . . business interests in New Jersey and Pennsylvania." He paused to let it sink in. As much as he talked about time pressure, he didn't seem to be in any hurry. "As you might imagine, the duties of house counsel are somewhat less defined than those of an outside attorney. I am called upon to give counsel and assist my clients regarding many varied situations, as you are."

"Were."

He frowned and nodded in sympathy. For a moment he nearly had me believe he was sincerely concerned, but his eyes betrayed him. They were as cold and hard as the muzzles of .45s. I wondered how many times he'd ordered men killed; I took it for granted that he had. Sometimes as we talked he seemed to see me. Other times he looked right through me, as if I'd already been dismissed. At that moment I wasn't there. "Yes, yes, I understand that the state supreme court was closely divided on your case. Correct?"

"Four votes for suspension, three for censure only."

"Sad, to be so close to success and have it slip away .Tell me, did you file for reconsideration?"

I wondered where the conversation was going. "For what it's worth. The review petition didn't keep the license suspension from going into effect. And they can sit on it for as long as they want. They've been sitting on it for two years already. From what my attorney tells me, in some cases they never act on petitions for reconsideration at all."

"Does your attorney have influence with the court?"

"He's a specialist in supreme court appeals; he's very knowledgeable about the personalities on the court."

He waved his hand in a small dismissive gesture. "No, any good technician can do that. I mean influence. Perhaps if someone would intercede on your behalf, behind the scenes. You only need one vote. And besides, even among the majority, there may be a feeling that now you've suffered enough."

It took a few seconds for the implications to sink in. They could even swing the vote of one--or more--state supreme court justices? Even though the room was well heated, I put my hands around the coffee cup to keep warm. I tried to keep my voice level. "What do you have in mind?"

"It has been brought to my attention that you're investigating the disappearance of one Daniel Wilson."

"That's correct." Theoretically, this was a breach of my duty of confidentiality. Under the circumstances, the theory took a back seat. Playing stupid with this man could conflict with another duty the investigator owes the client—staying alive to see the case through.

"Concern has been expressed," he said slowly, measuring out his words, "about the appropriateness of such an inquiry."

"I'm not trying to find who killed him."

"Oh?"

"Just to establish that he is dead. Are you familiar with the presumption of death arising from an absence of seven years?"

"Your inquiry is part of a civil action, relating to his estate?"

"The hearing is Monday afternoon in Montgomery County, in the Orphan's Court Division. The issue is whether a life insurance policy is payable."

"Who is your client?"

"I'm working for Wilson's estate."

"But who, exactly?"

I decided I'd said enough. He didn't seem to know as much as he pretended "The estate itself is a legal entity. It's my client."

He smiled again, and I began to sweat. "You know, it's useless to take such a position. We've had you under surveillance."

He was temporizing; two could play. "I'm surprised you tipped your hand by picking me up. You could have followed me on my rounds today."

"Come, come, Mr. Garrett. We knew last night you were conscious of us when you ran the tollbooth."

"I spotted your people even earlier." I looked at my forearm and read off the plate number.

He tried not to be impressed. "Even if that is the correct plate, you could have seen the number this morning and guessed that it was the same vehicle as last night."

"I was brought to the car from the front. Pennsylvania cars have only rear plates. And it wouldn't be written on my arm."

He wasn't ready to concede the round. "Why did you tip your hand and let us know you knew you were being followed? You forfeited an opportunity to sow false leads. Plus, you should have known we would react."

"I was on the way to my house. I didn't know if you knew my identity. I couldn't take the risk of taking them home if they didn't know who I was already."

I was hoping he would tell me I'd guessed wrong, that they'd known my identity last night. Then I would have known that they'd been tipped off. The only people who'd known last night that I was on the case were Jon Franklin, Harry Ziemer, Leo Strasnick, and Mark Louchs. And Lisa Wilson, for the sake of completeness. But my luck wasn't running, or perhaps he saw the trap.

"Let's get back to the subject under discussion," he continued. "My clients are concerned about the reexamination of closed business. They have some instructions for you."

"I'm listening."

"Stay on the Wilson case if you wish but, forgo any inquiries regarding the precise circumstances of his disappearance. To put it simply, go through the motions. The outcome of this civil case is of no concern to us. In return, we can advise you regarding the retention of a new appeals counsel to work with your present attorney. Someone who will be listened to when he speaks."

"'Or?'"

"There is no 'or', Mr. Garrett."

"I have a proposal of my own."

Something flickered across his face, something like interest. He waited for me to speak. I decided to ease into it slowly.

"It's safe to say that Mr. Wilson was not the victim of a natural catastrophe."

"That would seem a reasonable inference."

"More particularly, this was not random or accidental."

"I would tend to agree."

"Therefore, it happened for a reason."

"If it was not an accident, it would have been deliberate."

I took a chance. I had nothing to lose, and I couldn't see walking away. "Now, correct me if I'm wrong, but there are two possible reasons for what happened. Either it was pure retaliation, or it happened while trying to acquire information."

"Go on."

"If it was retaliation, there's no service I can render. But if it wasn't . . ."

"You understand, I have no authority, and can obtain no authority, to discuss my client's affairs with you."

"And I don't want to know anything about them."

"Mr. Garrett, are you suggesting that my client hire you? I trust not."

"No. My proposal is simply that if I learn anything that would be of interest to you, I will pass it along "

"We have our own investigative resources."

"They haven't delivered."

"Do you think you can do better?"

"What do you have to lose?"

"It would be much simpler to have you off the case. Less risk." I couldn't tell if he meant resignation or death. "You're out to prove Wilson was killed."

"By his own hand. Or by accident. Or by disease. Or by person or persons unknown. There is no evidence who did it, if it was a murder, and I'm not looking for any."

He frowned. "You seek to introduce complexities. I dislike them. You recall how Alexander dealt with the Gordian Knot?"

"I think the better analogy would be the myth of the Hydra."

"Ah, a man of classical learning." His voice brightened but his eyes looked past me again. He seemed to be interested, but also thinking of something else at the same time. It was unnerving. "One of the labors of Hercules, was it not?"

"He had to kill the Hydra, a beast of many heads. When one was cut off, two grew back in its place."

"You're not suggesting that two investigators will come forward if you are removed from the case?"

"What we have now is a seven-year-old disappearance with no leads. No one's cared about it in years, and after Monday no one ever will again. But if something happens to me, the police will get interested—not only in my case, but in the one I was working on. If you say you don't like complications, don't create any."

He considered my point. It didn't take long. "Mr. Garrett, I am going to take it upon myself to deviate slightly from my instructions. I'm told that when you were in practice, you had a high reputation for reliability. I am prepared to take you at your word, for the moment. I will tell you this, and no more. We are seeking return of certain property. It is believed to have last been in the hands of Mr. Wilson. If your inquiries lead to recovery of the property, then my deviation from instructions will be forgiven. If you cannot recover the property, or if your conduct creates other difficulties, my client will take appropriate measures." He sounded as if he didn't care how it turned out. He handed me a blank card with five phone numbers printed on it. "I will be available at either of the bottom two; one is my cellular phone. Don't photocopy the card or write the numbers down anywhere else. And don't lose the card; all of the numbers are confidential."

My mouth was dry and I wanted a sip of coffee, but I was afraid my hands were shaking too badly to pick up the cup. I took the card without comment and put it in my jacket pocket.

"Good luck to you, Mr. Garrett." He didn't look up when I opened the door.

CHAPTER FIVE
Saturday, 1:00 P.M.

I caught a bus back to my office and looked at the questionnaire Lisa had filled out. Mainly I was interested in Wilson's best friend, Todd Brogan, and his former girlfriend, then Elizabeth Chatwin, now Elizabeth Dosterburg. I was able to reach them by phone. Todd lived only forty minutes away, in West Chester. He sounded happy to cooperate, but Sunday afternoon would be better because his oldest boy had a swimming practice at noon. I had barely walked out of a room with my life, and I was talking about swimming practice . . . We agreed on late Sunday afternoon at his home. Mrs. Dosterburg said she was available anytime; since she was further away, in Hanover, I decided to see her immediately. The turnpike would have been a few minutes faster but I decided to go the long way, on 30. I always enjoyed the countryside, even with all the leaves down and a few inches of snow. Especially Lancaster County. Chester County is well on the way to being one big Philadelphia suburb, and somehow, I'd never cared for York County. But Lancaster--there was always something to see. Forty miles of rolling hills, some with just farmhouses, some with little towns, and patches of woods in between. At one time the whole county had been forested; I was sorry I'd missed seeing it.

Hanover was a quiet town of red-brick houses about fifteen miles from Gettysburg on a road that lead nowhere. You only go to Hanover if you intend to. Her house was in the middle of a street of identical two-story row houses, each with a second-floor bay window. The street was well tended; the paint was fresh and many of the houses had white window boxes. Most of the houses looked like owner-occupieds, but there was also the inevitable beauty shop, a bar, and a corner mom-and-pop grocery.

I left my car across the street, not bothering to lock up. It was that kind of neighborhood. There weren't many left, and I liked the feeling.

"Mr. Garrett?" a thin, high voice called from her door. "Please come right in."

She was a plump, pleasant-faced woman in her middle thirties with blond hair cut too short and too much cheap jewelry. She was wearing a pink silk blouse with a high V neck that probably looked better twenty pounds ago. There was a black skirt, almost new, that was more in line with her present proportions. She showed me into the front sitting room and invited me to sit on the sofa.

"Can I get you some coffee? Some tea?" It was a polite question, but the way she said it, there was something riding on my answer.

I'd learned to accept anything offered; if nothing else, consuming it gave you an excuse to prolong the interview. "Coffee would be great," I said. "It's cold outside."

"Great." We had made some kind of deal and she was pleased. She disappeared through a door to the back. I noticed she was wearing high heels in her own house on Saturday afternoon.

While she was out of the room I got up and looked around. The furniture was obviously from somewhere else. It was old, in fine condition, but it was too big for the room; chairs were jammed against the sofa, the Oriental was tucked under at one end, and the side table almost touched the wall. Inherited, I decided. Like its owner, the house was trying to live just above its station. On the mantel was her wedding picture, showing a thinner and prettier Elizabeth, with a long blond mane, smiling at the camera, next to a thin, dark young man in a white tuxedo. He didn't seem to be smiling. I wonder if he'd suspected what was in store.

Before I could poke around any further she was back, carefully holding a silver tray in both hands. She moved as if it were a religious rite--which in a way it probably was. She'd been busy since I called. In addition to a silver coffee-pot, with matching silver sugar bowl and creamer, the tray contained two cups, spoons, cloth napkins, and an assortment of small pastries.

"Thank you very much. I appreciate your hospitality." I'd gulped a cheeseburger and a large order of fries in York half an hour ago, but I took the coffee and a pastry. I had a job to do.

"You're very welcome, Mr. Garrett."

"I also appreciate your seeing me on such short notice."

She nodded. "Your time must be very precious right now. I'll try not to take up too much. But before we start, just how can I help? I didn't see him for months before he vanished."

"I know. It's a matter of negative evidence as much as anything—"

"Negative evidence?"

"Sorry, that's really more of a legal term. What I mean is, this is a case of a disappearance. If a person disappears and is not heard from for a long enough time, the law presumes he's dead. Evidence that something didn't happen--that you didn't hear from him, and that none of your mutual friends did—is important."

"I see," she murmured. I could tell that she didn't, but at least it gave me a chance to start.

"How did you meet?" I asked.

"Work. I had just graduated from business college and I was working in Philadelphia as a legal assistant. My firm was in the same building as Daniel's."

"And when was that?"

"I thought you would ask that, so I looked it up. It was just before Thanksgiving, eight years ago."

"You two knew each other for a little more than a year before he disappeared?"

"Yes and no. We started dating within a few weeks, and we were serious by January. But we broke up that summer; it was August, not long before Labor Day."

"You have quite a memory."

"No, I have it all written down. And the date of our breaking up is in my mind anyway. We were going to use the Labor Day weekend to drive around and look at restaurants and reception halls for our wedding."

"I didn't realize that things had been that serious."

"That's quite all right. It's been a long time. And I'm married now, of course," she added. She looked down at her wedding ring as if she'd just seen it for the first time. "The engagement hadn't been formally announced anyway, and there wasn't a ring. It was more like something that we both based our plans on."

I had the feeling she had said the same words a thousand times already, to herself. "You mentioned you were looking up dates and things. Is there a diary?"

She shook her head. "Oh, no. I just keep my old appointment books. From when I was a legal assistant. I would write in things like if we had a date, where we went, if we saw a movie what the movie was, things like that. Nothing more at all."

She wasn't that good a liar. There was a diary, but I could probably pull out her fingernails before she'd let me see it. And if she was answering my questions honestly, it didn't matter. She wasn't the case, he was.

"Tell me about him."

"He was really a wonderful person. Always polite, attentive, a perfect gentleman. Very intelligent, well-read, well-traveled. But not arrogant; he could always laugh at himself."

"I've heard it said that he was depressed."

"He had his moods. More towards the end. He could be very withdrawn, and he wouldn't tell me what he was thinking. But he never lost his temper or took it out on me."

"You say he seemed more down later in your relationship?"

"Very much so. At first, he seemed so bouncy, so cheerful. You could see it in his eyes. But as the months went by, he started to brood. His moods would pass and for a few days, even a few weeks, he'd be his old self. Then they would start again. By the end he was down all the time."

"What was he worrying about?"

She met my eyes. "Mr. Garrett, I never had the slightest idea then and I don't now. I wish I did. Maybe I could have helped. I only know that he was terribly bothered by something. I pestered him to tell me, even more toward the end. I thought if we were going to be married he should share everything with me, that we shouldn't keep secrets. But he never said."

"Could it have been money?"

"No. He managed his money very well, from what I could see. He was very generous with me, buying me clothes and jewelry and taking me out to dinner. He treated me like a queen. But he was very frugal with himself. I only saw his apartment a few times; it was very--basic. We never stayed overnight there, and that was fine with me. It was so much less than he could have afforded. He'd worked his way through school, so he had no school loans. He once said he had enough money saved up to put a down payment on a house for us plus buy the furniture."

"Did he say where the money was?"

"Funny you should ask that. He was very odd about banks. As we got serious he told me about his finances, he volunteered everything I've just told you. But as far as where he kept his money, he wasn't very sophisticated. He kept it in cash in a safe-deposit box."

"Did he say why?"

"It wasn't not trusting banks—if he didn't he could have buried it somewhere, I suppose. He just didn't like people tracing what he did with his money. Tracing how he spent it."

"Do you know what he meant by that?"

"Not a clue. Except that he talked about it in a peculiar way. Not about how he'd spent it in the past, but how he was going to spend it in the future."

"Nothing more specific?"

"Well, he'd say, 'If I wanted to do something that cost money, I wouldn't want everybody knowing about it.' Does that make any sense to you?" she asked.

"Only if I had an idea of what he was going to spend money on."

"It didn't come up often; it was his money and we never got to the point of pooling our resources. Until we were ready to set a date, it wasn't my place to ask."

"Did he gamble?"

"Not at all. He said that trying cases was gambling enough. And he said that money easily come by would go just as easily. Or even that it could bring bad luck. We went to Atlantic City once; he let me go into the casino and he took a walk on the beach."

"Let me ask about some other things. Did he have a drinking problem?"

"He was a hard drinker; you might say. Most of the trial attorneys I've met are. He had a couple of drinks every night after work to relax--Scotch, mainly. On weekend evenings he might have a third drink. Or we might have a bottle of wine with dinner. But if we had the wine, he wouldn't order a drink, too. He liked his booze, but he never used eating as an excuse to sneak more alcohol."

She allowed herself a sad, rueful smile and tilted her head a bit, remembering. "I'm sorry, you must think that I spent a year cataloguing his personal habits. But when you're thinking of marriage you keep an eye out. Anyway, he never drank anything during the day, even on weekends. And I can't say that I ever saw him drunk. He used it to relax, nothing more. And because it was part of the image."

"Image?"

"The whole being tough thing. Like being a Marine or a paratrooper--he told me a story once about that; he said it was a true story. I think it described him well. Do you want to hear it?"

"Please."

She pursed her lips. "I want to be sure I get this right. It was just before D-Day, in World War Two. General Eisenhower is reviewing the parachute soldiers who are supposed to jump behind enemy lines. They're all big, strapping men, covered with camouflage paint and carrying their equipment; rifles and ammunition and such. He walks down the line and comes to a puny little fellow with glasses. He's almost buried under his pack and rifle. General Eisenhower looks at him and says, 'Son, do you enjoy jumping out of airplanes?' 'No, sir.' 'Then why do you do it?' 'Because I like being around men who do."

We both smiled. "He told that story once at a dinner party and one of the men thought it was a homosexual joke. It was one of the few times I ever saw him angry. I'm not going to repeat what he said--he used some words that night I didn't think he knew--but the essence was, it's not a story about sexual preference, it's about courage."

"This is a difficult question, and I don't want to embarrass you, but since the subject has come up . . ."

She pursed her lips and took her time answering; I wasn't sure if she was thinking about how to phrase it, or just remembering. "Dan was no caveman, Mr. Garrett. He was a gentle, considerate lover. He wasn't the kind of man who would ravish you at first sight."

For just an instant she flicked her eyes at me. "But if he had a little encouragement, if he felt secure, he was fine."

"It's hard to discuss these things with a total stranger."

"I don't feel that way toward you, Mr. Garrett. I find it very easy to talk to you, as a matter of fact. I'm very much at ease."

I just nodded.

"By the way," she said, "Since we're speaking about sex, can I tell you something?"

"Please."

"He liked photography. Portraits. He had a couple of very nice cameras and some indoor lighting equipment. He kept everything at my place. He loved taking pictures of me." A smile began to form, and she looked away, just a little.

"Pictures?"

"Oh, nothing X-rated. But R, if you know what I mean. I'd be wearing lingerie or a pair of stockings. Or nothing at all. Very nicely done, with soft focus and pretty lighting. He had a real gift, he made me look so glamorous. I told him he could have been a photographer for *Playboy*. He just laughed." She played with her wedding ring.

"Did he ever sell any of the photographs commercially?"

"Lord, I don't think so. That certainly wasn't the idea. It was private, just for us. Just think of all those men looking at me." Her voice trailed off and she fingered the top button of her blouse. "When we broke up he gave me back the pictures. He said he didn't keep any. My husband made me throw them away." A sour expression crossed her face.

"That shoots down a theory I was working on. Well, not working on, but one I hadn't eliminated."

"Oh?"

"That he might have been gay, in the closet, and somebody was trying to blackmail him."

She laughed. "If you saw him on the street you might have thought that, just by looking. He was a . . . mild-looking man. But no, he certainly wasn't gay."

"I'd like to ask you about the photography some more. Did he sell other pictures? Or do work for people as a photographer?" Maybe he'd taken a picture or seen something he shouldn't have.

She shook her head and dropped the hand that had been playing with the button down to her lap.

"No, not that I know of. It was just a private hobby."

"Did he like being a lawyer?"

"Oh, yes. But he was willing to admit that he was scared before starting a trial. Most trial lawyers don't talk about that. They love to talk about how they outsmarted the other side, or how they worked hard and found new evidence, but they never talk about being scared. Not everyone likes being reminded."

"Did he take any drugs?"

"He'd smoked marijuana in college, but he stopped when he got to law school. He said it made him feel too dopey. There was never a suggestion that he took anything else. We were only together a couple of times all weekend but I'm sure I would have noticed."

"He didn't usually stay with you on weekends?"

"No, we used to fight about that, as a matter of fact. He'd spend every spare minute he could with me Monday through Friday, but most weekends he liked to be by himself. I told him that I felt like a weekend widow and we weren't even married."

"What did he do?"

"He said he was traveling. But he never took me along."

"What do you think?"

"Well, he was never home; I checked on that. But where he went, or if he was alone, I don't know."

"Could there have been another woman?"

"I've thought about that a lot. Then and later. But he told me I was the first woman he'd dated in more than a year. When he talked about his past, there had been a few women, but I never saw him as any kind of womanizer. If there was someone else, I never had a clue, and believe me, I was looking."

"I talked to a neighbor who said he sometimes saw a blond woman, well-dressed, around the place. Not all the time, but both before and during the time you two went out."

She was quiet, and then she shook her head. "He practically lived with me during the week. I can't see how there could have been time for anything serious, unless she was out of town somewhere. When things got bad I asked him if there was another woman; I told him he should be honest with me. He swore that there wasn't."

"Do you have any idea who the blonde was?"

"You sure you're not thinking of big sister?"

"She's not blonde. I met her this morning."

"Not naturally. But Dan kidded her once, when the three of us were together, about how she'd gone to nursing school and turned blonde. I guess she must be a brunette again now."

"Did he talk about his family much?"

"Talk about them? Oh, yes. We saw his mom almost every week. They were very close; and when Lisa was in town he'd take off a couple of days to visit with her. I liked Lisa, but I never got to know her very well. She only visited twice when Dan and I were together, and she and Dan spent some of the time together without me. But it always seemed like a happy family to me. His mother was very proud of them."

"Did he have many friends?"

"A few, but they were good friends. The kind of people you could always count on. The way he made friends, I thought it was a good sign he would be a good husband."

"Can you remember any of them?"

"The only one whose name I recall is Todd Brogan. He used to live in West Chester. I can't remember his wife's name, but they were a very nice couple." She hesitated. "Dan must have decided that things weren't going to work out months before it ended. He stopped introducing me to his friends." It seemed to be something she had just realized, and it hurt.

"But I thought you said you were looking for places for a wedding reception."

"I was. He wasn't. I could feel him slipping away, you see. And I loved him. I really did. I thought that by pressing for marriage I could put some momentum in things. He went along, but his heart wasn't in it. The next week I got the letter."

"Letter?"

"Telling me it was over."

"What did he say?"

"Would you like to see it?"

"Please." I almost didn't care if it was going to be a waste of time. Dan Wilson was a shadow. I wanted to touch something he had touched. If he was dead he was dead; I just wanted him to be more real.

She went upstairs and returned with a small white envelope. Our fingertips brushed as I accepted it. I could feel her eyes on mine, cool and appraising. The top button of her blouse was undone now.

The letter was handwritten on plain ivory stationery. The writing was small and clear. It looked familiar. I wondered where I'd seen a sample of his handwriting.

Dear Liz,

*I'm terribly sorry, but it's over. I've come to realize
that this just isn't going to work out. It's not anyone's
fault, least of all yours. But it's time to face the truth. I
have to do things that don't involve you or anyone
other than myself. And if you have a chance for
happiness with Bill I don't want to stand in your way.
I'm grateful for the fun we had together. You'll
always be remembered with fondness.*

Love,

Dan

I handed it back. "Did you speak to him about this afterwards?"

"Yes, but it didn't add anything. This is as much as I know."

"You say this was about four months before he disappeared?"

She nodded.

"Did he contact you again after this letter?"

"I phoned him after I got it. We talked just that one time. He was polite, and we worked out returning some things to each other, like the photos of me, but I knew he wasn't going to change his mind and I didn't try."

"Who's Bill?"

"My husband. We were married the fall after Dan disappeared."

"You were seeing him and Dan at the same time?"

"There wasn't anything physical till after Dan and I broke up." She leaned back in her chair and a little sideways, I wasn't sure if she was getting more comfortable or looking for a position to show her breasts to best advantage. "I didn't know the reason, but I was worried, for a long time before it ended that it wasn't going anywhere."

"Dan knew about Bill."

"I told him. I wasn't going to try to keep it a secret."

"Did you have a fight about it? Was that why he wrote the letter?"

"He took it well; too well, if you ask me."

"It didn't make him jealous?"

"I was hoping it would. When it didn't, I knew for sure it wasn't going to work."

"You're aware of the circumstances of his disappearance?"

"The police questioned me."

"Are you in touch with his family or any of his old friends?"

"No. We really didn't have any mutual friends, they were either mine or his. As far as family, I went to his mother's house, no one would answer the door, but I think she was home. Then I wrote to Lisa and to his mother; expressing my concern. I got a note from his mother thanking me. That's been it."

"You've moved and changed your name, if he wanted to get in touch with you, would he know how to do it?"

"If he called my old office, anyone there could tell him where I am. Or if he called my parents."

"What do you think?"

"He had a lot of cash. The stuff in his apartment wasn't worth anything. He was really unhappy. He had little to lose. He knew a lot about criminal law, how investigations work. He knew what they would look for."

"You think he decided to disappear?"

"I feel certain, I just don't know why."

I stood up. "Thank you for your hospitality. And if I find something out, I'll certainly let you know."

She put her hand lightly on my forearm as we reached the door. "I appreciate that your schedule is tight just now. If you'd like to call again feel free."

"The case will be over, one way or the other, on Monday."

"No matter."

I'd been propositioned a few times in my life, not nearly enough, and never so elegantly. But Mrs. Dosterburg wasn't for me. Even if she lost the pounds and grew out her hair, there wouldn't be enough room in bed for her and me and all her dreams.

"I won't forget that. Oh, and one more thing," I said as I put on my coat, "You mentioned that Daniel knew a lot about--how did you put it--criminal law and investigations?"

"That was what he did. High-level drug cases. And white-collar crime. I'm sure you know what I mean."

"Was that what he always did?"

"Not when he started practice, I don't think. But when I knew him."

I hadn't been on the case twenty-four hours and already I'd been lied to. Suddenly Mrs. Dosterburg and the touch of her hand seemed a long way away.

"Thank you very much. And now I need to run. I have to see someone in Philadelphia right away."

She said something more, but I was already crossing the street.

CHAPTER SIX
Saturday, 3:00 P.M.

Strasnick's house was what I expected, an elegant turn-of-the-century mansion on the Main Line with a long driveway to insulate the owners from the madding crowd. I wasn't expecting two matching new black Mercedes sedans in the driveway or that the door would be answered by a maid. At least she wasn't black or wearing a uniform; even ostentation stops somewhere. I think.

No one had answered when I'd called his office. Finding him at home was a calculated risk. And as good as any, since I had no place else to look.

The maid was more of a cleaner than a social secretary, or maybe she just assumed I was expected. When I gave my name, she showed me through a white-tiled foyer, through corridors and rooms all the way to the rear of the house and knocked on an oak door. She withdrew, taking my overcoat with her.

"Come in."

The room was small but paneled in oak to match the door. There were no windows. The brass chandelier above my head was turned off; a small brass reading light on the desk threw a pool of light on a scattering of documents. Strasnick looked up at me over his reading glasses. He was wearing a dress shirt and a tie, but the collar was open and the tie pulled down.

"You're working hard, Mr. Garrett."

"So are you."

"It goes with the practice. Never enough hours in the day."

I sat down without being invited. He regarded me from across the desk. "What can I do for you Mr. Garrett?"

"Stop the damn lies."

He didn't blink. "Concerning?"

"Wilson's practice."

"I thought I'd already made that clear."

I tried to keep the anger out of my voice. "And what was your understanding of what you told me?"

"General practice, with an emphasis on trial work," he explained patiently.

"Not criminal?"

"A few DUIs."

"And how does that differ from your practice now?"

"Mainly in that we can afford to be more selective in our choice of clients. I thought it was a simple enough explanation."

"Mr. Strasnick, I know a lot of attorneys in this area. I know a lot of people that did private criminal work seven years ago. As a matter of fact, I know several people who were assistant district attorneys back then. I can find out exactly what kind of trial practice Wilson had. I'd prefer to have you tell me yourself."

"I trust you're not threatening me, Mr. Garrett."

"No."

"Or thinking I had some role in his disappearance?"

"No."

He stood up. "Then I will have to ask you to leave. You're not my client, I have no obligation to talk to you, and I have nothing more to say. The maid will see you out."

I stayed sitting down. "I have it on very good authority that at the time he disappeared his practice was almost exclusively organized crime. Are we going to talk, or do I have you subpoenaed to testify on Monday?"

"What do you mean, subpoenaed? I'm not under suspicion."

"No, but with the circumstances surrounding his disappearance, I'm sure the judge would find it highly relevant that he—and his firm--had ties to the mob." It was my turn to stand up. "The hearing's at one-thirty in Montgomery County Common Pleas. I'm not sure of the courtroom; it'll be on the subpoena. Oh, and if

Monday doesn't suit you, if you can't make it, no problem; we'll get it reset for your convenience. After all, you're a key witness."
I started for the door.

"Mr. Garrett, please sit down."

I stopped near the door but didn't turn around. I didn't want him to see my face. I didn't know how I was feeling at that moment, satisfied or disgusted. I wanted to keep it to myself.

His voice was soft and careful. "I can see we need to discuss this further."

I sat back down and waited. He leaned back in big swivel chair and pressed his fingertips together. "This is going to take a while to explain. Want a cup of coffee? Or something to eat?"

"No, thanks."

"Look, Dave--can I call you that--I hear you used to be a lawyer yourself."

"News travels fast."

"Stories like yours do. I remember reading about it at the time. It's the kind of thing that sticks in your mind. But I didn't realize it was you till I saw you. I didn't feel right, bringing it up." I wondered where this was going.

"Tell me, what sort of practice did you have?"

"At the end, mostly personal injury."

"Were you with a firm?"

"After the first few years."

"I don't mean to pry but if your early days were like ours, was it rough going at first?"

"If you mean did I nearly go broke, yes. What are you asking for?"

"Dan and I went through the same struggle. Let me guess how it was and you tell me if I'm wrong. You're a brand-new lawyer. Neither a claimant nor an insurance carrier will hire you for civil lawsuits because you have no trial experience. The clientele you attract is mainly criminal matters. Correct so far?"

"Yes."

"The typical criminal client is a lousy credit risk. He has no money for a serious retainer. He's probably unemployed and already having trouble meeting his child support obligations, and he has those because his personal life is a mess. So, you take the case with a small retainer and hope he'll come up with the rest. Promises and promises, sometimes a few dollars when a court appearance is at hand. Once the case is over, your claim for a fee is a total write-off, no matter how hard you try to collect."

"That all sounds familiar."

"How did you solve your problem?" he asked.

"Once I got trial experience I was able to diversify a little. Some domestic, some landlord-tenant. Enough to get by. And then I got my offer with the firm."

"Suppose that during that difficult first couple of years a client had come in on a criminal matter. A different sort of client than you'd ever seen. Older than the kids you normally represented, better dressed, with a--shall we say complex--criminal record. He says he needs to beat the charge and wants your firm because he's heard you have the talent. He puts a cash retainer on the table that's as much money as the firm has taken in during the last two months. He says he'll pay more for a good result. And when your partner--Dan--gets the result, he doubles the retainer in gratitude."

"You must have known what you were getting into."

"Not right away. We just thought it was luck. But suppose you were in this situation and in the months that followed, you got a stream of referrals from this man, people who were willing to pay almost any fee for good results, and who gave huge retainers anyway? Suppose your firm's income went up tenfold in six months?"

"Then I would say you were bought and paid for."

"There was never a contact with--what shall I call it—the referring organization. Just individuals showing up by themselves. We never learned anything about how we were selected for the first client or how, exactly, they decided to keep sending people to us. And it was never homicides, all narcotics, RICO, embezzlement, extortion, arson, some prostitution, things of that nature."

"What would Dan have known?"

"Exactly what I told you. The clients never discussed anything but the facts of the case with us, not a one. It was better for everyone that way. There was never any one case that screamed out 'organized crime.' Nothing but the sheer number of cases. And there were never any big publicity cases; neither Dan nor I was ever in the newspapers. Everybody wanted it quiet, and it stayed that way."

"Who did the work?"

"We both did, at first. Then the firm started to diversify, just like you did. I handled the new matters and he concentrated on servicing the criminal clients. And very successfully, too, I might add."

"Was he ever threatened by a client?"

"No. Not, at least, that he told me. I'm sure he would have told me."

"Or by anyone on a client's behalf?"

"No. I told you, there was no contact. And the people we were dealing with had realistic expectations. If there were no deals to be made and the case went against them, they were at least satisfied that he'd given them the best defense possible. We never heard a complaint."

"At the time of his disappearance, what kinds of cases was he working on?"

"I checked when I heard that there was going to be a hearing. I have it written down somewhere, but there was nothing out of the ordinary. There were about fifty active files. Around ten felony drug cases, another ten were misdemeanor drug cases, half a dozen each of assault, Uniform Firearms Act violations, RICO, and soliciting. The rest were a little of everything--a few divorces, custody, personal injury, even a zoning case."

"You told me the last time we met that he seemed dissatisfied. Is there anything you'd like to add now?"

He seemed puzzled. "How do you mean?"

"Did he like the work?"

"Neither of us did, if you want my honest opinion. With the regular criminal trade, they may have been slow pay, but they were usually poor souls. You could feel sorry for them. You hoped that if you got them off they would straighten themselves out. You could think that you were helping them get a second chance, sometimes. These people we're talking about--well, they didn't stir those emotions."

"Did he want to quit?"

"At times, we both did."

"What happened?"

"Each time we would talk about it and decide to hang in a little longer. We could afford to hire associates. And we could afford to try these cases, the ones we're talking about, in the grand style. If we wanted to hire psychologists to help us pick jurors or fly in an expert from out of state or have expensive exhibits constructed, money was never an object. Just one example: in a drug case we might say that a certain toxicologist at the University of Illinois might be able to help us, and an envelope with the cash would be delivered the next day."

"Were you afraid to quit, back then?"

He shook his head. "We discussed quitting, but we never tried, at least when Dan was around. We decided that our imaginations were getting away from us if we thought they would compel us to take cases we didn't want. And that turned out to be true. They wanted good representation, but there was no reason it had to be us. There were lots of other hungry lawyers. Still are."

"But you couldn't have known then that they would let you go so easily."

"No, we didn't. And frankly, Dan was never as convinced as I was that they would. Let me tell you what I told him. The organization went to great lengths never to deal with us directly. We never learned anything about them—we weren't privy to any trade secrets. They were deliberately keeping us at arm's length. If we left, no information went with us. They could afford to let us go."

"And?"

"We were right. After Dan disappeared, I discussed the matter with the associates--there were no other partners then--and we decided to get out. We sent away the next three cases and we never heard from them again. My associates reported to me that a firm in Chester picked up the representation of all three."

"Why did Dan's disappearance make the difference?"

"Because it scared the hell out of us. First, if it was a homicide, we had no idea how it related to our organized crime representations. Or even if it was. We didn't know what to think. Was it a dissatisfied client from the organization? We'd never heard a complaint. Was it another client? Possibly. Could it be the organization itself? That didn't make much sense, because they kept right on sending us clients all along. But nothing seemed out of the question. One of the associates even suggested that two groups were involved, and that Dan had somehow been caught in the middle. It was as likely as anything else. We felt we were in over our heads. And if it was a disappearance, well, that sent us a message, too. Whether it was a suicide or a charade to cover his running away, it told us about the stress involved."

"What do you think really happened?"

"I'm sorry I lied to you about Dan, but I--well, let me explain it this way. You were a partner in a firm?"

I nodded.

"Then you'll know what I mean. You're with them eight, ten, twelve hours a day. You may not be on the same case, but you're always together. You see a lot more of them than you do your family. And they become like a family. tell me, are you married?"

"Divorced."

"Then I'll ask a different question. When you and your wife were in trouble, who did you tell first?"

"My partners."

"Even before your family."

I nodded again.

"Dan was more to me than an ordinary partner. We'd started it all together, sweated out meeting payroll, the whole thing. I was shocked when he left without telling me, but I respected his decision. And to be very candid, I wanted to protect him in this. I owe him a lot. I didn't want anyone trying to find him. So, I hid his motive to disappear and I told you I thought he was dead. I'm sorry I did that, but I hope you can appreciate my reasons."

"Where is he?"

"I have no idea. Dave, let me tell you something else. I told you yesterday we were doing badly when he left. That wasn't true. He lived simply; he could have saved up money like crazy before he left. There would have been more than enough to travel on."

"How much?"

He thought about it. "We took out the same. I was married, my wife didn't work, we had two small children. Even I was able to save. Dan could have saved enough to go to Arizona or Mexico or somewhere, maybe take a low-visibility job, and not have to worry about money for a long time."

"Is there any evidence he's alive?"

"No. He went to a lot of trouble to disappear in a way that would make them think he was dead. If the situation were reversed, I'd keep my head down, too, and hope that my friends understood."

"Has the insurance company subpoenaed you?"

"I told them I wouldn't be a cooperative witness."

"Why?"

"Because I really don't know what happened; it's just guesswork. The judge can guess as well as I can. And because I don't want to get killed."

"Go on."

"The organization doesn't like publicity, especially publicity that suggests they were involved in murdering someone."

"Have you been threatened?"

"They don't need to. It's obvious enough. And even if I'm wrong, I'm not going to take a chance. If this hearing means the company having to pay the money when he's not dead, I don't care--not when my life and the lives of my family are in the balance. If the company pays, we get a check from them and endorse it over to his estate. If he's not declared dead, there's no check for us to sign. It doesn't matter to me or my firm one way or the other."

I looked at my watch. I was already late for my appointment with Mrs. Wilson. "Anything else you want to tell me?"

He grinned just a little. "If you run into Dan, give him my best."

"I don't think I'm going to have the pleasure."

"No. Probably not." His smile disappeared. "Listen, I want to apologize about yesterday. It's not like me, and I didn't like doing it. I made a mistake about you."

"You could have saved me some time."

"If you were me, you'd have covered for your partner, too."

I couldn't argue with that. The late afternoon traffic was light as I headed east. Wilson's mother lived in Overbrook, a section of the city that was too tough to die. Hemmed in on all sides by the slums of west Philadelphia, Saint Joseph's College, Saint Charles Seminary and Lankenau Hospital, it never gave up. The big brick houses never deteriorated into warrens of tiny apartments; instead, they were bought by yuppies and renovated. The apartment buildings never went condo. The neighborhood stores stayed in business. It wasn't as pretty as it had once been, or as safe, but it was still a neighborhood. Mrs. Wilson lived in a brick row house between a funeral home and a drycleaner. The front porch had been enclosed with glass to create some extra space. Judging from the panes, probably in the late Fifties, and it looked like the last renovation the place had seen.

When I knocked on her door the peephole opened. I introduced myself and the peephole snapped shut again. The door remained closed for the better part of a minute. I heard two female voices. I couldn't get the words, but they seemed to be arguing. Finally, a couple of bolts drew back and the door opened.

A grim, matronly woman with steel-gray hair tied back in a bun confronted me just inside the door. She had a broad, Slavic face, dark and intense. Her eyes hinted at Asia even more strongly than Lisa's. Even though she was broad and no longer young, she carried herself with authority. This was her home.

"Hello, Mrs. Wilson. Pleased to meet you."

"You're here about Dan." Her voice was flat and cold as a frozen lake.

"Yes, ma'am. I expect Lisa told you. I've been hired by your lawyer to get to the bottom of this."

"Well there ain't no bottom to get to. He's been dead these past seven years."

"Perhaps we could sit down and discuss it for a minute?"

Instead of answering, she turned on her heel and walked through a doorway to her left. I couldn't tell if she intended me to follow or if she was just walking away. I followed and found myself in a small living room, spotlessly clean. It was a fussy, feminine room, done in soft peach, with lace trim on the sofa pillows and knickknacks on all the horizontal surfaces. I tried to keep my elbows tucked in. The room wasn't huge, but it wasn't small enough to explain my feeling of claustrophobia. The house was a place where time seemed to stop. I wondered if anything had been changed since Mr. Wilson died. Nothing I'd seen would have looked out of place in the Sixties. It made me want to open a window.

Mrs. Wilson sat in a wing chair. Lisa got off the sofa when I came in and offered her hand. "Mr. Garrett, how are you?" She had changed into a long black skirt. I wondered if her mother approved of her daughter wearing pants in her house. Mrs. Wilson looked like a woman with a long list of things she disapproved of.

Lisa smiled at me, doing her best to balance out her mother. Her palm was moist and her movements were awkward. I wondered how long she had been home and how much of the time had been spent arguing about my visit.

"Ma'am, I know this is difficult, but I need to talk to you about your son."

"No harder now than then," she said flatly. "He's dead, simple as that. Can't you understand that?" She looked at Lisa, expecting her to support her, but Lisa wasn't going to contribute to the argument no matter what she thought privately.

"I'm sure it's clear enough in your mind, but we have to convince a judge. The only things he'll know about the case are the things that come out in court. Your lawyer has asked me to help investigate."

"You might as well get on with it if this is costing me money."

I took a breath. "When did you last see Daniel?"

"The day he died."

"Where was that?"

"Right here."

"What time?"

"That morning. I don't remember exactly."

"What were his plans?"

"Didn't you already ask her all this?"

She was right about that. Dealing with this woman was so aggravating it was hard to think clearly. "Did he seem despondent or out of sorts around the time he disappeared?"

"No. And why do I have to keep telling you, he's dead."

"What makes you say that?"

"His car was found empty, shot full of boles, and full of blood. Don't take a lawyer to figure that one out."

"Do you have any other reason to think he's dead?"

She gave me the kind of look normally reserved for morons and said nothing. "Look," I persisted. "Do you still have any of his things?"

"Threw them all away."

"Do you have a recent picture?"

"That's a dumb ass question."

This woman was getting under my skin. "I mean, of course, from just before his--death."

"No."

I persisted. "Have you heard from him?"

"No."

"Are you in touch with any of his old friends?"

"No, and if he got in touch with them, I think I would know about it."

"Ma'am, I'm working for you, trying to help you--"

"Then find his body and leave me in peace! That's the only thing you can do that would be any good to me."

"I'm sorry. I know how this must hurt. Thank you for your time."

Lisa showed me to the door. "I'm sorry about Mom," she whispered. "She's never gotten over it. Dan was her only son, and he was the baby of the family."

"It must be hard."

"She's going to hurt anyway. Talking about it doesn't make it all that much worse. It may even help."

"I think she would disagree."

"It's partly my fault. I'm the one pushing the case. I had to twist her arm. She's suspicious about the money. Thinks it would bring bad luck. She's very old school."

"I'm going to guess that the name wasn't always Wilson."

"Grandpa Warniack got off the boat and decided they were going to be Americans." She stood a little closer and turned her face a little. "What do you see?"

"I'm guessing, eastern Poland."

"Anything else?"

I studied her face, but I wasn't sure what she meant. "No."

She seemed to like the answer. "You've had a busy day, Mr. Garrett."

"I'm on a tight schedule and it's not over yet."

"Now where?"

"I'm going to meet with Chief Ziemer again. Maybe look at the scene with him."

She wasn't pleased at my response. "I thought you were done with that."

"I'm sorry about the added expense, but I need to do this case my way."

"It's not the money. Just why go back there again?"

"Something funny is going on. When I went there last night a car followed me. They were from organized crime. After I met with you this morning they brought me in for a talk. They seem to think I'm trying to find out who killed Dan."

Her brow furrowed. "But you're in the case for a limited purpose, aren't you?"

"That's one of the things I had to explain to them."

"Did they want you off the case?"

"Not after I talked to them. But that was their idea first."

"They threatened the last investigator, didn't they? That's why they dropped us."

I didn't know what Mark had told her. Knowing Mark, he had probably concocted something. "I don't know."

She frowned at my answer but didn't press it. "Why don't you drop it?"

"It pisses me off when people think they can tell me what to do."

"I'm glad we have you on our side. Be careful." She smiled. "And sorry again about Mom."

CHAPTER SEVEN
Saturday, 8:00 P.M.

I drove away and stopped at Lankenau Hospital. The days of a phone booth on every corner are gone, even downtown in major cities. Looking for a public phone that works is a crapshoot. But hospitals always have phones.

I reached Ziemer through the department radio paging system and told him I had some new information. He agreed to meet me at eight that night at the scene. It was nearly six-thirty when I reached my apartment. No one seemed to be following. I looked around quickly and satisfied myself that the place hadn't been searched. After throwing a couple of pieces of pizza in the microwave, I changed into the clothes I'd worn the night before: jeans, a work shirt, and my parka. I was out the door again, the pizza on a paper plate, within ten minutes.

The turnpike unfolded under my lights as I rolled west. As I ate with one hand, I tried to make some sense of it all. Twenty-four hours before, I thought the possibilities were either a disappearance or a mob execution. Those were good starting points, and the investigation was supposed to be narrowing. Having talked to everyone there was to talk to, except Brogan, I was no closer to eliminating either possibility. I even had Ziemer's random killer theory to consider, and the possibility that it was a revenge killing by a disgruntled criminal client unconnected to the organization. The case was still moving in the wrong direction.

I hesitated, now that I had cleared things with Strasnick, to think that anyone was lying to me. I don't assume that everything that doesn't check out a hundred percent is a deliberate lie. Now that he had come clean about Dan's practice, Strasnick had no motive to lie about anything else, at least no financial motive. And why shouldn't Mrs. Dosterburg tell the truth? She was even less affected by the outcome than Strasnick. Unless she had told me some half-truths to get me to come back again . . . It didn't seem likely, but I'd never spent a winter in Hanover.

The Morgantown exit came up. I was ahead of schedule, and the pizza was sticking in my throat. I hit the drive-through at the McDonald's and ordered a Coke. As I waited I started thinking about the past. My ex-wife and I had been here before. The first time she took the bar exam, right after she finished, we booked a room at the hotel next door to celebrate. After all, who ever really flunked the Pennsylvania bar exam? It was the middle of August; the weather was breezy and warm the whole weekend. We rode around the farm country in Amish buggies and went to Gettysburg. We ate bland Pennsylvania Dutch food in family-style restaurants with improbable names like Plain & Hearty and Amos' Country Cookin' that were really owned by Jews from New Jersey. She left her diaphragm at home and packed her most wicked black-lace negligee; she wanted to launch her career and our family at the same time.

I threw the empty cup into the trash and put the car into drive.

I drove up Route Ten past the scene, checking for a tail. Then I hunted around till I found the road that led up the bank on the west side of the highway. It was a small dirt road, partly overgrown. If the ground hadn't been frozen the Civic would have been stuck for sure. The side road started on the right-hand side of Route Ten about a quarter of a mile north of the shooting. It climbed the bank in one steep swoop and then ended in the large flat area I'd been on the night before. No one was there, and in my headlights all I could find was the single set of tire tracks that led to the spot where they had watched. I drove back down again and waited.

Eight-thirty had come and gone when the chief pulled up. "Sorry to be late now. Had an accident to work near Birdsboro."

I told him about the other car, leaving out the plate number and the fact that I had carried a gun. And my conversation in

Philadelphia that morning. I finished with a very short version of what Strasnick had told me. Come to think of it, I didn't tell him very much. I hope it was enough to shake something loose.

"Well, now," he said when I was through.

"It's a heck of a thing." I offered.

"Yeah. Ain't it, though?"

I looked down and kicked the dirt. In my experience, kicking the dirt is essential when dealing with the Pennsylvania Dutch. Long silences also help. And if the conversation is about buying something, squint in the sun and shove your hands in your back pockets.

"Well," he said at last. "What do you think now?"

"I think it was a Mafia thing," I said. "I don't know why the body disappeared, but I can't explain otherwise why they would be so interested."

"Well, that could be," he conceded. He wasn't ready to give.

"Tell me, what did you find out about the victim's background, as far as what kind of lawyer he was?"

"That wasn't my case, back then. If Dietz didn't check it out more thorough, then he didn't. We were both sergeants then, but he was senior. I used to give him advice, but he didn't want to listen. As a matter of fact, I told him he ought to call down to the district attorney in Philadelphia and ask around about this fella. He said he'd done it. Looks like he didn't."

"Would you're getting to be chief have anything to do with his moving away?"

"That was his call. Anyway, looks like he wasn't too careful back then."

"Don't know where it would have led, if he'd checked."

"You know, though. This does explain one thing."

I tried not to sound too interested. "Oh?"

"The sister. Now, I expect family to be real upset when this stuff happens, but I get the feeling from talking to Dietz that she was worse than normal. Why, she was too scared to even get out of her car. She made him interview her in the car. Dietz didn't put that in.

He said afterward that it made him look too much a softy. He felt real sorry for her. We all did."

"Did she say why?"

"Just scared, she said. I guess of the Mafia, now that I've heard what you said. You talk to their mom?"

"Couple hours ago."

"Tough old bird, ain't she?"

"I've gotten more cooperation out of alligators."

"She was the same with us. Called us a bunch of fools for not catching the killers but wouldn't help us an inch. Wouldn't even give us a recent picture. Said it wouldn't do any good anyway."

"Think she was scared, too?"

"Nah, just contrary."

I waited, but the chief had exhausted his store of information. "Tell me, Chief. What ever happened to the car?"

"Still around," he said vaguely.

"After all this time?"

"It ain't in no impound, after all this time. But we didn't let 'em junk it out. You never know."

"I'd like to take a look, if I may."

"If you don't mind doin' a little drivin', I suppose there's no harm. Just don't sit inside. The stateys say they're working on some new tests that might show something new."

"Like what?"

"Couldn't say. I think they just want me to keep my nose out of the case. They figure they can solve it themselves."

He gave me directions to County Line Auto Salvage. I knew the area.

"Thanks. And like I said, if I find anything out I'll let you know."

"I'd appreciate that." He was too courteous to mention that it was the law.

"One more thing, Chief, while we're here. Can you help me place exactly where the car was found?"

"I didn't see it myself, but Dietz and I walked the site when there were still tire tracks from the Pinto and he showed me. Here, let me get my flashlight."

He went back to his car and produced a flashlight half the size of a baseball bat. Ziemer was no small man, but I could see from the way he carried it that it was heavy. Until they were banned, the Philadelphia police carried flashlights like that. They were basically clubs that also happened to throw light.

Our cars were parked just off the road. He led me down the trail until we were at least twenty yards from the road and shone the light on the ground. "Right about here now." I looked back. Route Ten was visible if you looked directly west, but thick trees pressed close on both sides.

"The pictures didn't show this well."

"I think the stateys towed it out to the road to take their pictures. Couldn't get good light on it back here. Trees were too close in on either side to set up the floodlights proper."

"Well, isn't that something." I said.

"What's that?"

"Lisa said she saw the car as she drove by on Ten. She couldn't have."

The chief wasn't impressed. "Remember that seven years ago these trees were smaller. And there would have been fresh tire tracks leading off the road in the snow up to here."

"The side windows were shot out. Where was the glass?"

"From the driver's side, a lot of it stayed inside. But the passenger's window went outward, all over the place. There was a bunch on the main road a few yards south of the lane."

"Do you know if the glass was visible?"

"I didn't see it myself. But Dietz said it was real sparkly, real visible. That's how he was able to find the little lane here."

Gritting my teeth, I started back for the main road. "Chief, is there any evidence in this case that's inconsistent with any of the ideas about what happened?"

"Don't feel bad. We've had seven years and you've had two days."

We stood beside our cars. "Headin' home now?" he asked.

I spoke as casually as I could. "It's not too late yet. You know, what you told me about the sister's got me thinking. I think I might just stop by her place." I wanted to keep the police advised of my movements. I just didn't tell him that she wouldn't be there.

CHAPTER EIGHT
Sunday, 2:00 A.M.

Lisa lived in the coal regions. It was sad, worn-out country, full of dead hopes, slag piles, rusted machinery, and hills that yielded vistas of nothing at all.. The towns were half-empty, and the people that remained were mainly the old and those unwilling to take the inevitable beating on the resale of their houses. To the extent that the area still had an economy, it was largely fueled by money earned by men who lived in New Jersey or Philadelphia during the week, six or eight to a motel room, then came home on weekends to drink it away and beat up their wives and each other. I was glad it was dark; I only needed to think about the dirty snow piled high on each side of the highway.

North Carbon, where Lisa lived, was in the heart of the region, a few miles north of Pottsville between two ridges. Some Philadelphians confuse Pottsville with Pottstown, a bustling and prosperous neo-suburb between Reading and Philadelphia. No one who has been in coal country would make that mistake. The town's last real prosperity ended with the Korean War. It looked neglected and tired; there was nowhere to go but downhill, and the town knew it.

I was hungry, and the only thing open was an old hotel with a gravel parking lot full of pickup trucks and motorcycles. A half-dozen men in baseball caps and work boots were going up the steps, and I decided to stop. I rolled down my window and caught the heavy, pleasant smell of frying hamburgers. Then they turned and looked at me. I knew the look and what it meant; I started the engine and kept moving.

Near the edge of town, I found a convenience store with gas pumps. The young girl behind the counter, who paid no attention to me, must have weighed two hundred and fifty pounds. She had the oily skin and flat hair of the morbidly obese. Her hands were still pretty; I found myself wondering what she'd be like without the weight.

"Got any hot dogs?"

"Just durin' the day," she said indifferently.

"Anything hot at all? It's sure cold outside."

"I shut off the stuff at five."

"Could you make me up a sandwich?"

She gestured vaguely around the shelves. "We got lotsa candy bars." It was true enough. I picked out two and a can of soda.

"Say, would you know a Lisa Wilson? She's supposed to live around here. Dark hair, middle thirties?"

She never looked up from the register. "Nah. I don't pay much attention." She was starting to breathe hard from the extended conversation. I picked up my change and left. Back in my car, I opened one of the candy bars, thought about the clerk, and decided I wasn't that hungry after all.

According to the address on the questionnaire and my road map, Lisa lived on the main road, two miles west of town. I picked my way carefully around the largest potholes. Once I had to go completely onto the shoulder to avoid a trench formed by a string of three large potholes that would have blocked a small tank. I began to appreciate the advantages of a pickup as my Honda bottomed out for the tenth time.

The road twisted and climbed, trying to escape the narrow river valley. There was no sign of life on either side except for occasional junked cars. Then, just as my odometer showed two miles, a light appeared on my right. It was a porch light for an old brick farmhouse. The mailbox said WILSON in two-inch high gold decals. I drove by slowly, taking my time. The house was facing the road, cut into the side of the hill, with the driveway on the side. No garage. No fence. The house wasn't large, and the porch light was big enough to illuminate not only the front porch, but part of the front yard, too. No sign of a dog, at least not outside.

I kept going until I found the next house, a rusting trailer half a mile further on. Wrecked cars were scattered about in various stages of disassembly. The trailer was tilted about ten degrees to the left and was leaning so far toward the road that I thought it could topple over at any time. No lights were showing, and in most places, I would have assumed it was abandoned junk. But when I used the driveway to turn around, I saw a dim light come on at the window.

I would have preferred to park my car away from her house, but there was no place any closer than town. Turning off my lights, I groped my way back down the hill until I could see her porch light up ahead on my left. Then I cut the engine and drifted closer. I rolled down the window and waited; there was no sound anywhere. Restarting the engine, I pulled into her driveway. Fortunately, she had shoveled it out. There was even enough room for me to turn around and point the nose of the car back toward the road.

I backed up as far as I could, nearly to the rear of the house. What was I looking for? I didn't really know. If Ziemer was right, Dan was dead. If Strasnick was right, he was in hiding as far away as a lot of money would take him. I had no reason to disbelieve either one. And even if I had, there was nothing to make me think he was in this little house in North Carbon in the middle of the night. But I was convinced that Lisa was hiding something. I had a hunch that the move back east had something to do with Dan besides being closer to their mother. Then again, my convictions weren't always the best guide. At various times in my life I'd been convinced that the Pennsylvania Supreme Court had a heart, that McGovern could beat Nixon, and that it would fall off if you played with it too much.

The real reason I was there was because time was running out and I hadn't the slightest idea what else to do. I climbed some steps to the back porch and found a rear door with a pane of glass in the top half. I shined in my pencil flashlight. It was the kitchen. The door was locked, but the lock was cheap. A couple of minutes with my picks and the door was open. A real pro could have done it in twenty seconds. I locked the door behind me and started looking around by flashlight.

The furniture, mostly dark wood Spanish pieces and a chrome-and-glass table, had nothing to do with the house. I suspected Lisa had brought it back from Los Angeles. The broad-plank pine floors were bare except for a few pseudo Navajo area rugs. Framed prints announcing LA art exhibits from years ago, appeared on several walls. Above the tiny brick fireplace, now in use as an outlet for a wood stove, were matching framed pictures of Lisa and her mother.

The layout inside was just four rooms. The front half was divided into a living room and a bedroom, the rear half was two-thirds a kitchen and one-third a bathroom. There was no upstairs or basement. The stove was out, but the house was still warmer than outside. I took off my parka and threw it over one of the chairs.

Starting in the bedroom, I went to work. In the corner was a small desk with four drawers. Not that it made much difference, but they were unlocked. I thought of all the times, as a lawyer, I had to obtain duplicate insurance policies, certificates of divorce, deeds, and car titles for clients who had misplaced them in their own homes and couldn't find them again, even with all the time in the world. But in the movies, the detective goes into a strange house, immediately goes to the correct floor, room, and piece of furniture, opens the correct drawer, looks briefly at one or two pieces of paper, and then finds what he needs . . . I was hungry already and I was going to be a lot hungrier before I had finished giving this place a decent going-over.

Being right-handed, and there being no better place to start, I pulled open the lower right-hand drawer. It contained some current ledgers and account books from a company called Pottsville Fabricating. The upper right-hand drawer was her liquor cabinet: a bottle of gin and a six-pack of small bottles of tonic water. In the lower left-hand drawer, I found her personal papers. The bills were the routine things: utilities, car repairs, car insurance, and a small MasterCard account balance. I went over the phone bills carefully. She had saved them for the last year and the only out-of-the-area calls were to Philadelphia. The number matched her mother's phone. The other listed calls were almost all to Pottsville Fabricating. No address book, at least that I could find. No letters saved from anyone. Her tax records for the last few years. Insurance papers for her car and medical insurance. Her canceled checks; except for some magazine subscriptions and a few small checks to people I couldn't identify, the checks that didn't match up with the bills were mostly to the Pottsville supermarket. Last, her bank statements, showing her biweekly salary as her only deposits during the last year. No mystery about where her money was going or where it was coming from.

The upper left-hand drawer was storage. The top item, in a black imitation-leather presentation case, was her nursing diploma from a Los Angeles hospital. Tucked into a corner was a snapshot, yellowed and creased, showing her in a nurse's uniform standing in front of a palm tree--a graduation shot, I guessed. It was over-exposed, and her face was in shadow, but it was definitely her. Next was her high school diploma. At the bottom was her passport, issued four years ago. The photograph showed Lisa deeply tanned, her hair pulled back, and smiling. The only stamping indicated a trip to Mexico shortly after it was issued.

The dresser was a cherry lowboy with six drawers and a large mirror. Except for a vibrator under her lingerie and an un-opened box of condoms, I found nothing but clothing. The bathroom medicine cabinet was small and crammed with lipstick, makeup, cleaning solution for contact lenses, cold remedies, and the like. No tampons. A bottle of generic aspirin and a half-used carton of generic antihistamines. One toothbrush. The only razor was a woman's model for leg hair. No evidence that someone else lived or even visited here. I was thinking about whether I should bother to search the kitchen when I felt a draft on my neck. Had I left the back door open? Before I could turn around, something exploded in the back of my head. For an instant I was in searing pain as I fell forward. I barely remember my head hitting the floor.

At first. I was aware of roaring in my ears. Was I at the beach? I seemed to be floating, but it was cold. And when I tried to move my arms, nothing happened. Still, the feeling of floating persisted. Then gradually—I don't know how long--the roaring faded. Through a red haze I saw a couple of dark objects. After a while I recognized them as my boots. I tried to move them and couldn't. Then I noticed that they weren't just brown; they were spattered with red. I started to feel the pain.

"Hey, Red, I think he's coming around."

"No shit."

Even when I kept still, the back of my head throbbed. When I tried to turn I felt I was going to pass out. I had a deep burning sensation all the way across my forehead. The taste of blood was strong in my mouth, and either my lip or my tongue was bleeding. The right side of my chest ached, and a knifelike pain ran across to the center of my chest if I took more than a very shallow breath. It was hard to breathe any deeper, anyway, because my stomach ached. Repeated blows to the solar plexus, I thought.

The lights were all on. Two men. Not the two from this morning. Bikers. Late twenties. Red was heavyset with a black tangled beard and heavily tattooed forearms. The other was tall and balding, with a Fu Manchu mustache. He wore a chain around his waist and carried a big hunting knife in a sheath on his belt loop. Both wore black Harley-Davidson T-shirts and looked mean as hell. Not just bikers. Pagans.

I was in the kitchen in a chair facing the rear window. My hands were tied behind me and my feet were tied to the chair. Gritting my teeth against the pain I looked down, flecks of blood were all around me. They'd tied me up and worked me over while I was out.

Red stood in front of me. Very deliberately, seeking the best footing, he took a stance with his feet wide apart. When he was satisfied, he put on a leather studded glove. Seeing it made me forget what I'd been through so far; one good swipe would take half my face off. The silver studs glinted in the light. He looked at me in satisfaction and pounded the glove into his palm.

"Ready for some more fun, asshole?""

I opened my mouth to speak and found myself just spitting blood.

"Jesus, Red, ease up," the other called.

"Fuck off!"

"Fuck you! You off him before he talks, you're gonna answer for it, not me, asshole."

"You need your fuckin' ass wiped."

"I don't need any trouble with the law or anybody else. We got no protection if we don't follow orders. And if my parole gets violated I'm back in Huntington. You, too."

"Let's do him the way we did that cunt who was hitchin'."

"That doesn't get what we need to know, fuckhead."

"You're so goddam smart, huh?"

"Let him come around and think about it. Then the propane torch."

"No shit."

"Do to him what he did to that snitch. Took him all night to die. This guy will spill if we give him time to think."

Red nodded and grunted. Reluctantly he took off the glove, though he couldn't resist kicking me in the shin as he walked past. The pain tore right up my leg to my hip. For a second I thought he'd broken my leg. I was nauseous, whether from fear or pain I couldn't tell. My only thought was that I didn't want to die that way.

The bleeding in my mouth was slowing down, and I was able to feel around with my tongue. I'd bitten into my lower lip, maybe when I was falling. Or when I was hit afterward. My hands and feet were securely tied, and I was so weak and hurting I probably couldn't have stood up anyway. They had probably done this kind of thing before, who knows how many times. All I could do was turn my head, slowly, and try to think. The house was in shambles. They were searching for something, as I was. Unlike me, they didn't care who knew about it. Every stuffed piece of furniture bad been slashed open, every poster torn down, every drawer turned upside down and dumped on the floor. Their boots made crackling noises as they walked from room to room, trampling everything underfoot.

They wanted information. I didn't know if it was about whatever the mob lawyer said was missing, or whether it was about Dan

Wilson. It wasn't going to matter which, because I couldn't give them anything on either one. It didn't even matter if they believed me, except that they would probably kill me quicker.

The only person who knew even generally where I was, the chief in Powell Township, had probably gone to bed a couple hours ago. No one was going to miss me until I didn't show up in West Chester for my next witness interview tomorrow afternoon. He wouldn't think anything of it. He would probably be glad I wasn't cutting into his weekend with his family. The first people who would really notice were Mark Louchs and Lisa, when I didn't show up Monday afternoon. I would have a good excuse, being dead for two days.

I became aware of another type of crackling sound, higher in pitch and sharper. Tapping on glass. There, at the rear window, was Lisa. Or at least I saw something, and I thought it was Lisa. I didn't know if she was real or I was just hoping. In the dim light, with the dark behind her, she seemed to be floating in the dark. I so very much wanted to believe she was real.

Not daring to turn my head too fast or too far, I looked around. Red was in the bedroom, tearing drawers out of the dresser. The other was in the living room. I looked back at her. She was holding up one finger and her eyebrows were raised in inquiry. Ever so slightly, I shook my head no.

Two fingers.

Yes.

With the two fingers spread in a V, she pointed to the right, toward the bedroom. I shook my head no.

One finger pointed to the bedroom.

Yes.

One finger straight ahead, toward the living room.

Yes.

She pointed with two fingers, once at the bedroom and once at the living room. I nodded. Then she brought up her other and showed me a revolver. It looked like a toy, but it looked a lot better than a propane torch.

She stepped back slightly from the window; we settled down to wait. It wasn't long. From the bedroom, Red yelled, "Hey, come see this!" I don't know what caught his attention, but the other ambled in. I looked at the window and nodded. No danger of being surrounded. They were both in the same room.

The rear door opened, and she crept into the kitchen soundlessly, wearing the same jacket and jeans I'd seen that morning. Up close, the gun looked like a .22. A bazooka would have been my preference. I was surprised she could move so quietly on the linoleum. until I looked at her feet; she was only wearing her socks, and they were soaked through. I wondered how long she'd stood there in the snow. She was a few feet to my right, holding the gun in front of her with both hands, when the two of them came out of the bedroom together. They were laughing about whatever they had found. They saw Lisa and the gun, and their laughter stopped.

"Hold it right there and put your hands up!" Her voice was nervous and diffident. She was shaking so badly the gun was dancing around. And she was holding it wrong--both hands wrapped around the grip, and her arms were fully extended, elbows locked. She was halfway to handing it to them. It made me wonder if she'd ever fired a gun in her life.

Once Red got over his initial surprise, he wasn't impressed, either. He looked like a man who had been in situations like this before and had lived to tell about it.

"Well, little lady, suppose you hand that over to me." He smiled and took a step forward.

She took a step back. "Stop right there."

He smiled more broadly and took another step. "Now you're not gonna shoot no one, lady. Just hand over that thing before someone gets hurt."

She shook her head.

"Come on now, baby." He was taking slow steps, but big ones, and he was right in front of me. No more than four feet from her. His hand was reaching out, almost touching the gun.

At that moment the world exploded. A thunderclap of sound and a flash of light leapt from the gun, and a neat black hole appeared in the palm of Red's hand. For an instant his arm seemed to deform and twist; I realized that the bullet had smashed the bones in his wrist and tunneled up his forearm. It must have ripped some nerves.

"Son of a bitch!" he yelped, and bent over, clutching his arm. The other one made his move. His knife was ready. He must have eased it out while Red was going for the gun. Crouching down, he shoved Red to one side and charged. He knew his stuff. He kept the knife low, not far above his knees but the point high. He lunged toward Lisa, aiming for her stomach.

There was another explosion next to my right ear. The round went wild. I heard the tinkling of glass somewhere. Then she fired again, hitting him in the shoulder. It didn't even slow him down. Now the knifepoint almost touching her. But she held her ground and fired again. This time she caught him at the point of his chin, causing his neck to snap back like he'd taken a punch. Blood spurted everywhere, and he went down. The knife clattered on the linoleum.

She moved the gun back to Red, but the fight was out of him. Judging from the blood, she'd hit an artery in his arm. He was pinching the entry wound in the palm shut with his good hand, but blood was spurting out an exit wound somewhere up his forearm. He couldn't compress both.

"Both of you, lie down on the floor in the living room."

Red helped his friend to comply. There was no argument. With one eye and the gun on them, she cut me loose. If there was pain when my circulation was restored, I didn't notice. She motioned to hand me the gun, but I shook my head; I was in no shape to take charge. She nodded and raised her eyebrows.

"Water," I croaked.

She brought me a glass. I sipped, rinsed out my mouth, and spit on the floor. The shape the place was in, it didn't matter much anymore. Most of what came out was blood. I sipped some more and spit it out; still lots of blood, but more water this time. I kept going until it was just water with a trace of blood. Then I poured the rest over my head. Diluted blood ran everywhere; my face must have been covered with it. I cleared my throat. If I kept my voice low and spoke slowly, I could talk, a little.

"Why shouldn't we kill you?"

No response.

"Better give us a reason. Who sent you?"

Silence. Just then I couldn't talk anymore. I nodded to her. Lisa walked over to Red, keeping the gun pointed in his face.

"This is my house you wrecked. Tell me who you did it for."

Red looked up at her. "You ain't gonna shoot a man in cold blood, lady."

There were three very surprised people in the room when she lowered the gun and very deliberately shot him in the kneecap. When the echo died away—even a .22 makes a huge noise in a confined space--she raised the gun again. This time she pointed it at his groin. Their eyes met; I wondered what Red was seeing in her face.

Her voice was quiet. "Who?"

No response.

She cocked the gun and started squeezing the trigger. He swallowed. "Guy with the mob in Philly. Don't know his name. We do jobs for them, muscle stuff, sometimes. He called and said to search the place and put the squeeze on anybody who was here."

She looked back to me, not moving the gun. I nodded. It was my turn.

"What else?" I asked. My mouth was bleeding again.

"Get rid of them afterward. But get the information first."

"What information?"

"Where the stuff was."

"What's his name?"

"Don't know his name. Never did. No bullshit. He doesn't know mine, neither."

"What were you looking for?"

"Fifty grand in cash. Fifty-fifty split if we found it."

"How do you know he's mob?"

"He's in tight with them. He's one of their lawyers."

"You sure he's a lawyer?"

"Yeah and he said he had suck with all kinds of people if we got picked up. So long as we did like we were told we didn't have to worry about the law."

My vision was starting to go, and the room was moving away. They might know more, but it was time to get rid of them.

"Very slowly, take out your wallets and toss them over."
I looked. I was not surprised to find about a thousand dollars in one wallet and eight hundred in the other. People like them had no credit and no bank accounts; and no legal explanation for the money they had. It was simpler to just carry it around with them.

"We keep the IDs. And toss me the truck keys. That's good."
I had to stop again to swallow. "Now get out of here before we call the cops and don't think about coming back."

They struggled to their feet. Lisa stayed clear of them and kept the gun trained.

"Hey, man," Red pleaded at the door. "You can't make us walk to town like this. Without our coats and my leg. It's miles. And it's cold. We could die out there."

Slowly and painfully I stood up. The room spun around me. With my hand on the wall for balance, I moved over until our faces were inches apart.

"I hope you do. Now get out of here or you'll die right here."

They limped out the door and down the driveway. I watched till they disappeared in the gloom in the direction of town.

"I can't believe you just let them go."

"On Monday, when the case is over, we'll drop the dime on them. You heard them, they're both on parole. We just don't have time to deal with them right now."

"You said that if—"

"I lied."

CHAPTER NINE
Sunday, 10:00 A.M.

It was the headache that woke me. When I opened my eyes it was light, but it took a while to orient myself. I was lying down. In her bedroom. On the bed, with the covers over me. It was warm and I could smell the close, pine scent of the wood stove. The sun was well above the horizon. The windup alarm clock by the bed said 3:30 and its face was cracked. I wondered what they thought could possibly have been hidden in the clock.

I turned my head slightly to the left, trying to minimize my movements. The pain in my head and ribs was bad enough just lying still. Something dark was lying on the pillow next to me. I started to reach for it with my left arm and found it blocked; something was lying across my chest. I felt around; it was an arm. I followed it across my chest, from right to left, and found that it ended in a shoulder pressed against my left side. I moved further and touched a breast. The arm stirred and squeezed me gently; then the dark thing moved--it was Lisa's hair--and her sleepy face appeared.

"How are you feeling?"

I moistened my lips. I tried to speak twice before I could get the word out. "Headache."

She got out of bed and for a moment I had a view of her back-- tanned, freckled, and muscular. She slipped on a bulky white robe. I heard the water running and she returned with a bottle of aspirin and a glass of water.

"Take two as a start" she said. "If that doesn't help take two more every half hour. Take them till either the pain goes away or your ears start to ring. Stop if you shit black; that means your stomach lining is bleeding."

The aspirin would take a while to work, but the water at least lubricated my throat. I struggled to sit up and found that I was naked except for some tape on my ribs. The knife-like pain of last evening returned when I moved too quickly. With her help I managed to sit up and get some pillows behind me. When I was settled she sat next to me.

"How are you feeling?" she asked.

"It's time to talk. You go first."

"You ought to rest."

"Talk."

"Okay. Hanging around Mom's was getting on my nerves. You saw how she is. Plus, I need to get our records at work to the accountant in the next few days. I decided to come home and work on the books today. I'm going away to Cancun for a vacation when this is over, so I needed to get this done." She brushed her tousled hair away from her face. "I drove up and saw a pickup truck in the driveway and the house lights on. I pulled in and didn't see anyone. Then I saw your car. They had parked the pickup sideways, so you were parked in. By then I was scared. I remembered what you said about being warned off. I tiptoed around the back and saw you tied up. I went back to my car and got the gun."

She saw my puzzled look. "It's just an old twenty-two that I got on a trade when I moved up here. I shoot snakes in the woodpile every now and then. I haven't shot it in a couple of years."

"You did fine."

"It's a good thing a gun works no matter how scared you are."

I nodded in agreement. I wasn't going to talk more than I had to.

"And it's a good thing the guy with the beard decided to talk. When I shot him in the knee that was my last bullet."

I had an image of Red, his blood up from being shot twice, finding out we were defenseless. Let alone the other guy. There must be a God, and he does love idiots.

"Oh."

"After they left you passed out. I got your clothes off and cleaned you up. You're lucky; nothing that needs a doctor. It looks worse than it is. You have a big cut on your forehead, a cut in the inside of your lower lip, some bruises, tenderness in the back of the head. Nothing that needs stitches. And some bruised ribs. But"--she smiled—"You already knew about those." She picked up my left wrist, placed her thumb against my pulse, and looked at her wristwatch for a few seconds.

"Your pulse is good."

"Clothes?"

"There's no washing machine here. I use a laundromat in town. I rinsed them out in the sink and hung them near the stove. They'll be dry soon."

"Good. Then we can go." I started to get up and was brought up short by the pain from my ribs.

"Easy. You shouldn't be going anywhere. You need some rest."

"The hearing's tomorrow."

"You've got yourself half killed over it. Isn't that enough? Let it go."

"This is bigger than your brother. It's still going on. Whatever it is, it's big."

Before she turned her face away I could see that it was flushed. "Just let it alone, will you?" It was sheer luck you weren't killed. You've learned a lot, more than enough to make the judge happy. It's not worth it."

"I'm going ahead."

"None of this will bring Danny back."

I took my time speaking. My headache was worse, and the room was starting to spin. "Either I'm crawling out the door naked on my hands and knees, or I can do this with your help."

"I'm worried about you."

"I'm safer with you to help."

She turned back to me. "Okay, you idiot. I'll help. If you promise to stay in bed till noon, I'll drive you wherever you want."

"You didn't ask me what I was doing here."

"I thought you must have decided you needed to ask me some more questions, and you found out I'd left Mom's."

"No. I wanted to search your house."

Her eyes widened. "To see if Danny was here?"

"Or a lead to where he was."

"Then--you didn't believe me."

"It's my job not to take things on faith."

"You mean, you thought he was hiding out with me? That I've been hiding him here all these years?"

It sounded stupid. "I didn't know."

"It's like Mom said. You're looking in the wrong place. Go to the swamps in south Jersey, or wherever they hide the bodies."

We hadn't talked more than a couple minutes, but I was tired already. Black spots started moving in front of my eyes. I nodded yes and closed my eyes. I'm not sure if she had time to get off the bed before I went back to sleep. When I woke up again, I smelled coffee and bacon. She came into the room in sweatshirt and jeans, her hair pulled into the braid hanging to one side and dragging a big plastic garbage bag behind her. My headache was only a little better; I took two more aspirin.

"You might as well take four. It's nearly noon."

"Is breakfast ready? Smells good."

"Been ready for an hour. Hey, hold it. Let me help you up."

By holding only my left arm, she was able to help me sit up without increasing the pain in my ribs. But standing brought on a wave of dizziness. The room spun around and started to go dark for a moment, and my knees buckled. She dug her hip into mine, judo-style, and supported me with her own legs.

The moment passed, and I was able to stand alone, with my left arm against the wall for balance. She helped me into her terry-cloth bathrobe and followed close behind as I worked my way along the wall into the kitchen. I ate slowly, afraid of not keeping the food down. I looked around. Lisa had a work ethic. Some of the wreckage had already disappeared, and the floor and walls were mopped clean of blood. The main reminders of the previous night were the ripped cushions and the bullet hole in one of the panes of the kitchen window.

"How's your head?"

"Still hurts. But I feel better with some food in me. Could you get me my clothes and the aspirin?"

Supporting myself against the kitchen table, I stood up while she helped me off with the bathrobe and then helped me dress. Even though I was as sore and dizzy as ever, I felt better in my clothes. They were rumpled, torn, not fully dry, and still bloodstained in places, but at least I was dressed.

"You're going to lie down again, I hope."

"It's nearly one. We have a long day ahead of us."

"Why?" She crossed her arms over her chest and glared at me.

"Because I have a job to do."

"A job? You know what your job is? To get on the stand and say that nobody's heard from Dan in seven years. Period. End of story. That's all you have to say to meet the burden of proof. Now drop it."

"Somebody thinks there's more to this case than a disappearance, and they're going to a lot of trouble to find out."

"Well, they're right, it is more than a disappearance. Dan's dead. It's just that there's no body. Everyone can see that. And besides, you're hurt."

"Like I said, you can drive me, or I'll do it myself."

"You are the most goddam frustrating stubborn man!"

"Then help me up. I need to pee stubbornly."

In the bathroom mirror, I studied my face. A gash clear across the forehead. Eyes sunken and bloodshot. The entire left side was red and puffy. And everything would probably look worse tomorrow. But my nose wasn't broken and none of the cuts were very deep. I thought of what I would have looked like after a session with the propane torch.

The food and the aspirin made my headache a little better. The dizziness was another matter. Every change of position sent things spinning. As carefully as possible I worked my way along the wall back to the kitchen and sat down.

"Lisa, come sit."

She sat across the table from me, still annoyed that I wanted to keep going. Before I started I took two more aspirin with the last of the coffee. I could feel a new headache coming on, this one in the front of my head. This one had nothing to do with last night. It had to do with right now.

"The night Dan disappeared, what time did you finish shopping?"

"I don't remember."

"Try again."

"It's been a long time. Can you remember what time you finished watching TV seven years ago?"

"You were at the Park City Mall in Lancaster."

She nodded slightly. She knew enough to be suspicious when people asked questions when they already knew the answer.

"Your dinner reservation was for what time?"

"I don't remember. Seven. Or later maybe. He made it, anyway."

"The restaurant says it was for eight."

"If that's what they say."

"It's an hour's drive from Park City to Morgantown at most."

"So? I mean, I think that's right."

"The police checked the purchase slips in your car."

"They prove I was shopping at Park City that day."

"More than that. Some have not just the date but the time."

I took a leap. "Lisa, if I told you that Park City wasn't even open past five on Sunday nights, would that help you remember?"

Silence.

Another leap. "If I told you that none of your purchases were after five?"

"Then I must have left earlier."

"Like five?

"Maybe. I don't remember."

"You told me it was a Saturday night. But it happened on a Sunday."

"What difference does that make?"

"The stores are open later on Saturdays."

"Whatever time I left, I left."

"And what did you do then?"

She weighed each word carefully. "Drove around and looked at other stores that were still open. Drove through the Amish country and watched the buggies going home after church services. I was just killing time till dinner. But so what?"

"There was an awful lot of time to kill between five and eight. There isn't a hell of a lot going on in Lancaster County on a Sunday night in the wintertime." It was time to press my luck. "A restaurant that fancy, most customers arrive early and have a drink at the bar while they wait for their tables."

"I wouldn't know what Dan had planned. He'd been there before, not me."

"You would have wanted to arrive at seven, seven-thirty?"

"I told you, I don't know."

"But the time all fits. You leave Park City at five, drive around for maybe an hour; plan to arrive around seven. I get it that you might want to stretch what could be a one-hour trip into two. You were on vacation. But no more than that."

"So?"

"You did something for the better part of three hours you never told the police about." Or me, either but I didn't say that.

"Now hold on a minute. Even if I left Lancaster at five, if we were going to meet for a drink at seven or so, that would only leave one hour unaccounted for--and I just told you what I did. Drove around."

"No. I mean what you did after the shooting."

Her face froze. I let the silence stretch out. She must have been breathing but I couldn't see her chest moving. "Lisa, you called in the shooting at ten-thirty. You never told the police exactly what time you found the car; but you gave the impression that it was around ten, or even a little after. But the shooting happened closer to seven than ten."

"How can I possibly know when that happened?"

"Because you were there."

"I told you--"

"I know what you told me and what you told the police. It doesn't make sense. If he was coming up from Philadelphia, he would have used the turnpike and taken the Morgantown exit. You say he was supposed to meet you right there. Why would he drive right past your meeting place and go up Route Ten by himself?"

"I have no way of knowing why. Maybe he wasn't coming from Philly. He could have been seeing a client somewhere else. West Chester or somewhere."

It was time to try another tack, even if it wasn't based in fact. "How did you spot the car? It was back in the woods so far it couldn't be seen from the road."

"Of course it could be seen. You say you saw the police photographs."

Sometimes a lie gets you to the truth. "The car had been moved. It was so far back in the woods they couldn't get the photos they wanted. With headlights shining on it, of course you could see it. But if you were driving by, your headlights wouldn't have picked it up. It was too far off the road and hidden in the trees."

"I told you, I saw it. That's that!"

She didn't mention the glass particles in the roadway. If she'd found the car the way she said, she'd have to know about them. I was certain now she was lying. "Lisa, you had to have been in the car. The person who was shot was the passenger, not the driver."

"What are you talking about?"

"The spatter marks from the blood prove it. And the car was moving when the shots were fired, so there had to be a driver. Plus, after somebody was shot in that car, someone was able to turn into that little side lane and get it stopped. Someone who was in good enough control to stop without hitting the trees on either side. Nobody shot with a forty-five at close range can drive that carefully." She shook her head, but I went on. "And if the driver wasn't hit, the passenger was. There never were two cars. You were both in the same car and you were driving."

"Why are you doing this?"

"Because Monday afternoon I have to swear to what I think happened. And I'm not going to help prove a case that he's dead if I think that the key witness isn't giving it to me straight."

Her face was still stone, but at least she was breathing again. I softened my voice. My headache was worse, and the room was starting to wobble even though I was still sitting down. "Lisa, you may not think so right now, but I'm on your side. You saved my life and I'm grateful. But we need to be able to trust each other. Come on now, come clean." She took a deep breath and looked down at her hands. I waited.

"Is what I say confidential?"

"Yes."

She spoke softly. "There was only one car. We were together. We left from mom's place late that morning, went to Reading then to Lancaster. We left the mall around five, drove around the Amish country like I said. I was driving because Dan was tired. He had worked all day Saturday. Then we drove to Morgantown and started north on Ten. It was a little before seven."

I nodded. "Go on."

"It was dark. A car came up behind us and started to pass. I remember thinking that they must either know the road well or be in a hurry because the road was so full of curves. Then as it pulled alongside us I heard a backfire, real close, and then another. I looked over. There was a passenger in the other car; his window was down, and he was pointing something at us. I didn't see what it was, but then I knew it had to be a gun. I couldn't tell anything about him except that it was a man. I yelled 'Duck' and tried to keep my own head down. Then there was a huge crash and my side window just disappeared. Glass was all over the place--in my hair, in my eyes. I jammed on the brakes. There were some more shots, I don't know how many. Just as I was getting the car slowed up I saw the lane and pulled in. The other car slowed down but then a couple of other cars came up from Morgantown and it speeded up and went out of sight ahead of us. I got the car into the lane as far as I could."

"It was only then you had time to look at Dan?"

"He must not have had time to duck. There was—there was a hole in the middle of his forehead. He must have been looking towards the other car. His eyes were still open; he just looked surprised. I think he died instantly."

"What happened next?"

"For a minute, nothing. I was just hysterical. Then I realized that they might be coming back for me. They must have seen that there were two people in the car, and they couldn't be sure they'd taken care of both. And I knew they weren't far away. There was nothing I could do for Dan. If there had been, I would have stayed. Or carried him, or whatever had to be done. But there wasn't. The cell phone in the car still worked. I called Mom and told her what had happened. Then I went into the woods to wait."

"She drove up and gave you her car."

"While she was on her way up I thought of a plan. It took her an hour to get there, so I had time to think. I decided to tell the police that I hadn't been at the scene. I knew that would get into the newspapers. When they—those people--read that I hadn't seen anything, I thought they might leave me alone. It was my way of telling them I wasn't going to say anything."

"You dropped your mom in Morgantown because you couldn't afford to have her seen."

"I left her at the McDonald's. So, I went back to the car. I was just going to get out my packages and put them in Mom's car. After all, I couldn't have explained how my stuff was in his car if we hadn't been together. But when I got there he was gone."

"Any footprints?"

"Just on the driver's side; nothing on his side. And I'd gotten out the driver's side myself. From the blood it looked like he'd been taken out the driver's side. Finding him gone scared me even more. They knew where the car was, and they'd been back. For all I knew they were watching me right then. I got my packages and got out of there as quick as I could."

"Then you stopped somewhere, washed up, combed the glass out of your hair and called the police."

"Now you know why I'm so sure he's dead."

"I wish you'd told me this before."

"I had to stay with what I told the police. Even now. What if they find out that I was an eyewitness?"

"I have to share this with your attorney. But I think we can win without having to disclose any of this in open court."

"We have to. I'm sticking to my original story. I'd rather drop the case or perjure myself than give them a reason to come after me after all this time."

"I'll make that clear to Mark." I was basically through with my questions, but I wanted to ease out of it slowly. Our nerves were both raw and I couldn't leave things like this. "What did Dan really tell you about his involvement with Mafia cases?"

"He never used that word. He was ashamed of that work. But sometimes when he'd talk about a drug or extortion or bribery case, you had the feeling that it was part of a bigger operation."

"Did he ever mention names or particular clients?"

"Oh, no. I don't think he could, anyway."

"Why would they have wanted him dead?"

"I don't know."

"Did he ever say anything to you to suggest that he was concerned for his safety?"

"That last couple of days we were together he seemed a little edgy, like something from the office was bothering him, but he didn't say anything. It didn't seem that big a deal, either; more like there was some misunderstanding with a client or someone that had to be worked out. But I'm sure he would have told me if he thought he was in danger."

It had been an exhausting conversation and I had managed to get a hundred yards further up the same blind alley. At least the aspirin were finally helping. And I found I was able to get up unassisted, if I braced myself on the back of the chair.

"Let's go."

"How do you feel?"

"Fit as a goddam fiddle."

"I doubt that."

"We're going."

CHAPTER TEN
Sunday, 1:00 P.M.

Gingerly I maneuvered my right arm into my parka while Lisa held out the sleeve. It was painful enough to convince me not to try to take it off again until I had to, but at least the ribs stayed where they should, under the skin and outside my lungs.

When we stepped outside, the afternoon was cloudless and cold. The tops of the pines were swaying, but in their shelter all we felt was a slight breeze. The driveway in front of my car was empty except for Lisa's car and a complex of tire tracks; the Pagans must have come back with a second set of keys while we were asleep or hotwired the truck.

"We didn't hear a thing," Lisa said.

"I know I didn't. I bet they pushed it up to the road and rolled it a ways before they started it."

"With his bad knee?" she asked.

"Breaks your heart, doesn't it?"

"Makes me wish my driveway was even steeper."

"I'm glad they've got it back. When they get pulled over for the parole violation I bet the cops find drugs and God knows what else. I don't think anyone will be seeing them for a long time. On the outside, I mean."

My first thought was to take my own car, but then I thought again. The boys in Philly knew the car. Lisa's might get past them.

My dizziness refused to go away, but I discovered that I could walk unassisted if I took each step deliberately, like a drunk trying to walk without a stagger. I went to my car, got out the .357 magnum and checked to make sure it was still loaded. Then I turned one of the pockets of my parka inside out and tore a one-inch hole in the lining. When I replaced the pocket and put the gun in it, the barrel went through the hole, and the rest of the gun fit comfortably in the pocket. I got out my camera and locked up the car again.

I got in Lisa's car, an old brown sedan with more than its share of body rust. She had seen the revolver.

"Where did that come from?"

"I keep it under the seat."

"What for?"

"Protection, if I'm ever confronted when I can't get out of the car."

"Why such a big gun?"

"If I'm ever in enough trouble to have to use a gun, I don't intend to show it first. A round this big will go right through the door."

I had to close the door with my left hand and finding a comfortable position was hard. I had to settle for a contortion that left me leaning to the left and half twisted toward the driver.

"Where to?" she asked.

"We're headed for a junkyard near Honeybrook, Chester County. For the moment, head for Reading. Take Route 61."

She pulled out and started down the hill toward town.

'What's the plan?"

"The car is in a junkyard, impounded by the police as evidence. I want to give it a look. And there's a friend of Daniel's I want to talk to."

"Why?"

"The car, I want to see it for myself. And take a few pictures. I can run them through a one-hour photo service on Monday and have some pictures for the lawyer to show the judge. Let him see for himself."

"Didn't the police take photos?"

"I told them I'd leave them out of it if I could. They gave me a lot of cooperation. Plus, if we subpoenaed the chief there's no telling what he might say. Especially if the insurance company's lawyers got lucky on cross."

"I don't understand."

"I don't know if he'd really do it, but suppose he starts rambling about how the case is full of loose ends and unanswered questions and how peculiar it is because they've always solved their homicides before. It starts raising doubts in the judge's mind about this disappearance."

"It's not a disappearance."

"But you're not going to be testifying."

"Don't they have to call me to explain what happened?"

"You mean, so you can say what you said to the police?"

"Yes."

"Like you said, that would be perjury."

"You wouldn't have this problem if you hadn't badgered me into telling you what really happened."

"You don't mean that."

"I said what I said, and I'm stuck with it."

"It's up to Mark, but I figure I'll testify about the car and the disappearance. Keep you out of it."

"But you weren't there. Isn't that hearsay or something?"

"Not if Mark qualifies me as an expert. Then I can give my expert opinion about whether there was a homicide and base it upon hearsay I've received from others."

"Will they let you do that?"

"In Pennsylvania, in a civil case, with no jury, almost certainly."

"So you need to see the car firsthand?"

"Just me. You don't have to see it."

She took her time answering. "It's just a car now."

"You can decide later."

We drove for a few miles in silence. My headache returned, but I got used to the idea of being in motion.

"There's something I should tell you," she said. "About my coming home last night. I did it to see if you would be looking around."

I hadn't quite accepted her story, but I was still surprised. "What happened to make you think I'd go to your place?"

"Nothing in particular. Just that Mom was so difficult and there was so little time and I could see how badly you wanted to get to the bottom of the case. It was just a feeling."

"Thanks for telling me."

"You know, I never imagined going through anything like last night. It's really true that you can be too scared to do anything, even if it means saving your own life."

"It must have brought back some memories for you."

"With Danny it was all over in a moment. This was something that I had to gear myself up for. Want to know something? Even if you hadn't signaled they were both in one end of the house, I was getting ready to come in anyway. I was afraid I'd lose my nerve if I waited any longer."

"Or freeze your feet off."

"I never felt a thing. Not numb, I mean; I just never noticed."

"You did fine."

"Once I fired the first shot, you mean. Before that I was too scared to even protect myself. From then on, I was rolling. Getting started was the hard part."

"You sure surprised Red, there at the end, shooting him in the knee."

"He made it easy. When he wanted to take the gun away from me, at first, he pretended to be so nice, asking me to do him a favor. And I knew it was bullshit, but I almost did it anyway. But later, when he was down, he looked at me the way he really looks at women. Pure contempt. We're all stupid cunts who need a man to slap us around and show us what to do. It's a good thing I didn't have any more bullets. You know, I scared myself that way, too. I really could have killed him. I mean, not just that I had a gun—I wanted to kill him, and I was in the mood to do it. Shooting him in the knee felt good. Too good."

"You're pretty hard on yourself, generally."

"What do you mean?"

"An attractive young woman, career of her own, making it in the big city, gives everything up to juggle figures in a backwater where the average age is sixty and where Red is probably one of the most eligible men around."

"So, it's not LA."

"It's not anything. What's up here for you?"

"You men. If you were told you'd have to live in my house alone for six months you'd be figuring out a way to get laid within two days."

"Hey, take it easy. You know I didn't mean it that way. It's just that there're no neighbors, no movies, no TV, no library. Nothing to do in town except go somewhere else. What kind of a life is it?"

"A quiet one. And a simple one. And it suits me fine."

"What happened in LA to change you? I mean, you must have liked it to stay for so many years."

"At the time, I did. But passing thirty, and Dan, and Mom being alone--well, LA suited me for a while and then it didn't. What can I say?"

We drove in a companionable silence for some miles after that. What could anyone say? At least she chose her own place instead of just staying on where she happened to be born.

My headache receded to the point where I could think about food again. We stopped for lunch at a Howard Johnson's about twenty miles north of Reading on Route 61. I sat across from her in a booth, still wearing my parka. I was vaguely nauseated, but I ordered anyway. Even sitting in the car, I had felt my blood sugar falling. I put some ice in my coffee and waited for it to cool.

"Mr. Garrett?"

"You've seen me naked and you saved my life. You should call me Dave."

"Are we in any danger?"

"Not from the Pagans. If they were going to come back, they would have rousted up their buddies and been around last night. But as for the people that sent them, yes. Not sitting here in the middle of a public place, and I'm pretty certain we weren't followed. But yes, there's risk."

"I've been looking in my mirror the whole time. I'm certain we weren't followed."

"I didn't want to worry you, but I've been checking, too. It's easy when you have to sit the way I do. But it's hard to be sure. Not seeing the tail is either good or very bad."

"Go on."

"The tail can be so good you never see it."

"How?"

"It's a question of resources and skill. A good tail might involve five cars. All in radio or phone contact. You have a close tail that keeps you in sight, and someone else farther back. They trade off every few miles. You have a car in front who can pull over and keep an eye out if the boys in the back lose touch. And he may drop back and trade off covering the rear himself from time to time. But my experience is, in a multicar tail, the man in front is usually in charge. You have the likely destinations staked out so that if everybody screws up or the suspect gets suspicious, you can pick it up again. If you're confident you know where the suspect is going you can have changes of cars waiting along the route, too, but that's pretty sophisticated."

"Have you ever done a tail like that?"

I laughed. "No, no. All I've done is read about them. They're expensive for private jobs. It's more of the kind of thing the government can do. But when there's a lot at stake, like the DEA following a courier in a drug case through a major city, it's done like that. The people I tail are mainly cheating husbands and wives going to visit their squeezes. All they can think about is how horny they are. I could probably sit in the passenger's seat and not be noticed. At least on the way."

She smiled. 'You've been an investigator how long?"

"Two years."

"So how do you know all this?"

"When I started out I did a lot of criminal work. You pick up a lot of police procedures. Then when I did personal injury work, I was the lawyer and the investigator rolled into one. The issues were mainly traffic accidents, but it got my mind working in the right channels. My domestic work involved investigations. And I had a lot of friends on the force, especially detectives. When I lost my license and told them what I wanted to do, they spent a lot of time answering questions. The rest is on-the-job training."

"How could you make friends with the police if you were a defense lawyer?"

"I was fair with them on the witness stand; never pulled anything crooked. I never made a claim I couldn't prove. And I never allowed a client to perjure himself. Besides, the lawyers that the police really hate are the DAs anyway. They see the defense lawyers as just doing their job. They respect them for it. But when the DA tells them he's dropping their prosecution they go apeshit. They think they've been stabbed in the back."

"You know your job very well, Dave."

"Not well enough. If I did, I wouldn't be sitting here hurting and I wouldn't have needed you to wipe my ass for me. I was sloppy last night, and it was pure luck it didn't get me--and you--killed."

"They caught you by surprise."

"Pearl Harbor was a surprise. That's an explanation, not an excuse. I should never have let it happen. But I was so far out in the woods and it was so late I got sloppy. I should have secured the door behind me--blocked it with a couple chairs or some boxes--and kept my gun with me. Simple precautions. But that takes thinking, and I'd shut down. I was too eager to see what was inside."

"Now you're the one being too hard on yourself. Didn't you lock the door behind you?"

"Sure. But your lock is so simple that anyone who seriously wanted in could have gotten past it."

"I couldn't have."

"It's the people who could get past that lock silently that you need to be scared of."

We paid our bill and left. Standing next to her car I scanned the parking lot carefully. I didn't see anything.

Somehow, I wasn't comforted.

The junkyard was on Route 322 a few miles west of Honeybrook, near the Lancaster County line. We were on top of a ridgeline, and the cold westerly howled past our ears. The sun was casting long shadows, but there was plenty of light left.

Ziemer's directions had been perfect. The junkyard was on the south side of the highway, about half a mile west of the Lanchester landfill. I was surprised at how small it was, not more than fifty or seventy-five cars, and no fence. No sign or office, either. The owner probably only dealt with people he knew.

I was ready for a conversation with Lisa about whether she was ready to see the car again, how she could wait, but she got out before it could happen. I guess she'd decided. We walked around until we spotted it, sitting by itself at the rear next to a line of hemlocks. Except for the rust, it looked much the same as in the police photos. Sheets of plastic had been taped tightly over the driver's window and the passenger's window. Walking slowly on the uneven ground, I looked at it from all sides.

"Why would they store the car out here and not at the police station?" Lisa asked.

"Takes up room. For a long time. And anyone who was interested in it for the wrong reasons would know where it was."

"But couldn't something happen to it out here, too?"

"Something random, sure. Someone could steal a wheel or something. But no one out here is going to want the fender or the important pieces. And even if they did, the police still have their pictures. Keeping the actual car around is just backup for a case that is almost certain never to happen."

As I squatted down to get a close look at the bullet holes, my dizziness returned. I closed my eyes and concentrated on breathing evenly, hoping Lisa wouldn't notice. When I was able to open them again, I saw that the edges of the holes showed the same angle that the strings indicated. The rounds had come from the rear and slightly above the fender. It all fit.

"Lisa, how fast were you going when the other car pulled up?"

"Forty, maybe a little faster. We weren't in any hurry."

"Did you brake hard?""

"Yes. But not to the point of leaving skid marks, if that's what you want to know."

"Did you brake before or after the shot that broke the window?"

"It happened so fast the shot was before I could get the car slowed down much."

I nodded and walked around the car again, taking pictures as I went. I stopped when I reached the rear. A small hole, not much bigger than a pencil, had been punched into one of the lenses of the taillights. Ignoring the dizziness, I got on my hands and knees to study it. The lens wasn't cracked around the hole; it was a clean punch. And from what I could tell the bulb inside looked intact. I took four close-ups and one longer shot showing the taillight and the license plate.

I checked the rest of the car and found nothing. We got back in Lisa's car. I told her to turn right and head for West Chester. Dusk was falling, and she switched on her lights.

"Where in West Chester?"

"I want to visit a guy named Todd Brogan. He gave me directions; they start once we get to town."

"Was he a friend of Daniel's?"

"That's right."

"Did you find anything back there?"

Normally I don't discuss investigations in progress with the client, especially when all I have is a suspicion. But this wasn't a normal situation.

"The left rear taillight has a small hole in it. I can't be sure, but I think it's old. From the time of the shooting."

"What does that mean?"

"It helps prove your brother was murdered by a pro."

"A hole in a taillight?"

"If you want to tail someone, and you're confident that they don't know they're going to be followed, you can make your job easier. You take a pencil or pen or something of that size and punch a small hole in the lens of the taillight. When it's on you see a small white light in the middle of the red. Then you can drop back farther and not have to worry about losing your man in traffic."

"Dan and I were followed all day?"

"Possibly. It wouldn't do any good in the daytime, of course, but someone may have followed you most of the day and done this when dusk was coming on. Look, you need to tell me exactly where you two went."

"I was staying at Mom's. He left from his place and came directly there. We had a late breakfast together."

"He didn't go to his office first?"

"No. It was a Sunday, and I was supposed to leave on Tuesday. He'd worked most of Saturday so that he could take the whole day off."

"What time did be arrive?"

"Nine or nine-thirty. We ate and left about ten-thirty or eleven."

"Did anyone know where you were going?"

"We told Mom I was going clothes shopping. I said 'the outlets' but not where. We could have gone to Allentown or somewhere in lower Bucks or even over to New Jersey for all she knew."

"Why was Dan going along?"

"It was our only chance to see each other. And he would shop for things of his own. Books, records, things like that. He collected photography books."

"So I heard."

"We went by the turnpike to the Ephrata exit and then went north to Reading. We shopped the outlets till two or three and then drove straight to the Park City Mall. We had a snack and shopped there till five, when it closed. Then we drove east on Route Thirty through the tourist area. We took back roads and watched the buggies for an hour. Then we cut north to New Holland and took the main road east to Morgantown. We got there a little after seven. I remember thinking we were in no hurry because we still had an hour till our reservation."

"Any stops after Park City? Even to use a bathroom or get gas?"

"No."

"When you were at Park City was your car in the middle of the lot there?"

"There were lots of cars and people around."

"That probably saved you two from getting killed right there. They probably had been following Dan since he left his apartment, waiting for their chance. The car wasn't alone until you got onto Route Ten."

"We were alone in the Amish country."

"Not alone enough. You think of Lancaster County as rural, but every square inch is in use. It's one big factory, but because it's a factory for plants and animals instead of machines, everybody thinks its wilderness. There are people everywhere--you're never out of sight of farmhouses or some little town. There isn't much secluded country unless you know exactly where to look. Too risky from their point of view. They'd waited all day they could afford to wait for a better opportunity. Especially because the car was so conspicuous with that taillight."

"Does the hole in the light help our case?"

"Maybe, but it's not as solid as you think. The insurance company's lawyer is going to rip me up on cross--it could have been put there yesterday; it could have been there because of some innocent reason, like a piece of gravel, a year before the shooting; it could be damage from the shooting. It could have happened any time in the last seven years. I can't prove that it was done the day of the shooting; that's the weak point. And the worst part is that the police didn't pick it up."

"So?"

"The inference will be that if they didn't see it then, it was because it wasn't there then."

"The feeling it gives me, that they were following us the whole time . . . It's creepy."

West Chester hadn't changed since the last time I'd visited. It was a slum trying to convince itself it was a suburb. As we drove through the downtown, a few trendy neo-Victorian shops with hand-carved signs thrust out at us from a background of grimy brick storefronts. We turned onto Brogan's street and parked in his driveway. It was a pleasant, middle-class neighborhood with old shade trees, generous setbacks to the houses, and no sidewalks. Brogan's house was a two-story brick colonial with well-tended shrubbery. And, I saw as I approached the porch, two days' uncollected newspapers. Going up the three porch steps brought on the dizziness again, and when I leaned against the wall I used my right arm by mistake. At least the pain from my ribs brought me back into focus.

"Go ahead and ring the bell if you want," I said disgustedly. "It isn't going to do any good."

After we satisfied ourselves that no one was home, I had Lisa walk around. I wasn't in shape for it just then, mentally or physically. This wasn't just a missed appointment. Someone had warned him off. I decided to keep it to myself.

"There's no car in the garage," Lisa reported. "A couple of inside lights are on in the back, plus the exterior floodlights. Everything is locked up tight. Looks like someone really didn't want to talk to us."

So much for keeping my own counsel. "Yeah."

"So now where?"

"Take me to a phone booth. We'll decide after that."

We retraced our steps and found a phone at a convenience store near Route 100. Lisa gave me all her change and waited in the car with the engine running. I let it ring twice, hung up, and called again. The phone was picked up, but no one answered. "'Yo, this is Garrett."

"From where?"

"A phone booth."

"Okay. You got the bucks, I got the dope."

"You really have something this time?"

"Don't bust my balls."

"One large," I offered.

"This is good stuff, man. You'll want to know."

"How good?"

"Ten large."

"You crazy?" I asked.

"No shit, man. I got expenses. This is a three-way split."

"I never paid more than three."

"I never had anything this good and I never had to go to this trouble."

"Four or forget it." I didn't mind the bill. It wasn't coming out of my pocket. But he expected me to haggle.

"I gotta pay two to the guy who told me. I need six, minimum."

"Five."

"When?"

"Tomorrow. The usual way."

"Okay. The dope is, Wilson was doing work for the big boys. Not an inside man but getting into some heavy cases."

"That much I knew."

"Fuck you, man. I bet you didn't know this. They offed him."

"'I've figured that, too."

"You don't know why."

"He'd taken something of theirs." It was important to make him think that I could find out a lot on my own, or his prices would go through the roof.

"But you don't know what."

"Fifty thousand in cash," I guessed.

"You don't have any background, do you?"

"That's what the five's for, if it's worth it at all. And if it turns out I'm paying this much for crap, this will be our last call."

"Hey, don't shoot off like that. He was doin' a case, drug case, for one of their people. The dude gave Wilson a bag with fifty g's in it for safekeeping. Then the guy gets killed. He's a middle-level coke dealer; one of his customers tried to strong-arm him and they shot it out. Wilson keeps the money, thinking nobody knows. But the big boys figure it out. End of story."

"You earned your money. But don't think that next time I'll pay five for the weather report. This kind of money is a one-time deal."

"Same for me, man. This is too heavy."

On that note, we hung up. I was tired and disgusted and in pain. My headache was back, and my food wasn't sitting well. And as I walked back to Lisa's car she had the lights on. I saw a white beam of light peeping out of the left rear taillight.

CHAPTER ELEVEN
Sunday, 6:00 P.M.

I got into the car as quickly as I could and hoped that no one had seen me break stride. I found myself touching the. 357 for reassurance. Hard thinking has saved a lot more lives than hardware, but the cold chunk of metal felt good anyway.

"What's the matter?" she asked. I didn't like the situation and I didn't like that she could read me so easily.

"Pull out slowly onto 100 north."

Evening traffic was heavy for a Sunday. I looked back and then in front, wondering which lights had our names on them. "Lisa, we've got a problem. Someone has marked our taillight, like Dan's."

"When?"

"I don't know. It could have been at the restaurant near Reading. We weren't watching the car every minute. Or it could have been while you were parked at my office yesterday. Or while you were at your mom's."

She looked in the mirror. "Is anybody following?"

"In this traffic, no way to tell. And if they're good, we'll never know it."

"What do they want?"

"They might want to kill us; they might be just following us to see where we go; they might be trying to sell us a subscription to Boy's Life. Let's work on the most pessimistic assumption."

"Okay, what do we do?"

"When you get to 30, turn left and head west, back toward Lancaster. We need some elbow room. It's too easy for them to follow us in traffic."

"But if we're alone with them?"

"We're going to have to stop sometime. And we sure can't go to my place or your place. Even if we lost them on the way, they may be staked out."

"What about going to the police?"

"If they would be so obliging as to pull in behind us when we get to the station, fine. But assuming they don't, then they just lose themselves until we come out again, what do we do? Hang around the police station all night and hope we don't get hit on the drive to Philly? Ask the police to stop suspicious-looking cars, whatever that means? We don't even know who to describe or how many there are."

"I still think the police could help."

"At most, and I mean most, they could stop one or two of the cars. If this is a serious tail--and there's no way of knowing how big it is--if we don't get all of them, then all we've done is make it worse. Right now, they don't know we're wise to them. If they mean us harm, they'd move in right away and the hell with the fact that there could be witnesses."

She was quiet for a while. "Okay."

"In your purse, do you have any cotton balls?"

"In my overnight bag. There on the backseat. In a little plastic bag along with my nail polish and the nail polish remover."

I fumbled around in the dark until I found them. I moistened four with my mouth, put two in my own ears, and gave the others to her. "What's this for?"

"Ear protection. Put them in."

"Okay, but why?"

I spoke slowly and carefully to make sure she could hear. "If something happens it'll happen fast. There won't be time to explain. If someone pulls up alongside who means trouble, I'm going to have to shove this gun right in front of your face and shoot out the window, past your head. I'll be firing a couple of inches from your ear. This gun is ten times more powerful than your .22. It's going to sound like the end of the world."

"This is like a bad dream I can't wake up from."

"At least this time we know what's coming."

The traffic thinned after we turned onto Route 30, but there were always three or four sets of lights behind us, plus a couple in front. Every so often someone would pass and my mouth would turn dry. I kept the gun in my lap, ready to shoot left-handed if necessary. A pair of hot-rodding teenagers came very close to death when they pulled alongside and matched our speed. Then the passenger smiled at Lisa and they pulled away.

We avoided the four-lane bypass around Downingtown and went through the city; it would be too easy to make a hit on a deserted, limited-access road.

"I've got a plan," I said, speaking a little louder than normal.

She was all business. "Let's hear it."

"We're not far from the Welsh Mountains. I have a friend who has a cabin there. He only uses it in the summers; I'm sure it's empty now. No one will be expecting us to go there."

"What's the Welsh Mountains?"

"In eastern Lancaster County, near Blue Ball. It's a series of wooded ridges, pretty steep by Lancaster County standards. Very undeveloped, or at least it was until recently. Very poor and remote area. Few roads. My friend's place is well hidden. If we can get there we'll be safe. And we don't have much choice."

"You think my mom's is being watched?"

"Probably. And even if they're not watching it now, you can bet they'll start if we shake the tail."

"Let's do it."

"Pull into the next self-service gas station you see."

"We've got plenty."

"We don't need to buy gas. This is about buying a few seconds. We can't lose them with the taillight as it is. Your nail polish, is it red?"

"Close enough."

"You're going to have to do this. I don't trust my balance. When we pull in, shut off the lights and get out. Take the nail polish with you. Start pumping the gas and open the trunk. Make like you're looking for something. The left lens is the damaged one. Reach inside the trunk and feel along the wires to the base of the bulb. Pull on the base till the bulb comes out. Then paint the bulb red; cover it completely. Then put it back in place. Be sure it's in solid. If the light doesn't come on, we'll be even more conspicuous. Pay for the gas and get back in. Start the engine but don't touch the brakes or turn on the lights. And buckle your seat belt tight."

"What's the point?"

"They don't know we're onto them. The tail may be loose right now. If they can't see their marker it may take them by surprise. If we can get ten seconds on them it may be enough."

Another five minutes up the road, at the intersection with Route 340, we saw a convenience store with pumps. The view ahead was good. I looked behind me as we pulled in; several cars went by. One pair of headlights pulled into a parking lot about a hundred yards back and went out. And up ahead, a car stopped just before the 340 intersection. He was good; he was positioned to follow us either way. I could feel the gun becoming slick in my hand.

Lisa opened her door and bounced over to the pumps as if her biggest worry was the amount of the discount for cash. She started pumping. Then, making a show of biting her thumbnail, she opened the trunk and rummaged around. For about a minute I heard nothing; Jesus, couldn't she find the bulb, or get it out? Then she paid for the gas and got in again.

"What went wrong?"

"Nothing. All done."

I let out my breath. "Thanks. Good job. Ready?"

She nodded.

"We're boxed in. There's one about a hundred yards back and one up ahead at the intersection. When I say, pull out and go down to the turn. Take it easy. After you turn onto 340 west, hit it and go like hell."

She started the engine and put the car into neutral. Her foot, I noticed, stayed clear of the brake. She was a good person to have in a tight spot.

Two cars passed by close together; five more were coming up. The gap was no more than three car lengths.

"Now!"

She slammed the car into drive, hit the lights and shot smoothly into the gap. The car right behind us honked, and my heart jumped. But the car I was really interested in, the one in the parking lot, was stuck waiting for the five cars to get by. If Lisa did the job right, we'd just be one of half a dozen sets of identical taillights in the dark.

I got a good look at the car up ahead at the intersection, a dark late-model Thunderbird. One occupant. Most likely the man in charge. Lisa slowed, made the turn without signaling, floored it, and dropped down a gear. The engine howled, and I was snapped back in my seat. My ribs hurt, again, but I kept it to myself. Behind me, I saw a single pair of headlights; the Thunderbird.

"We've lost the one who was behind us. He must have overshot the intersection looking for us."

The speedometer passed sixty and then seventy, but the Thunderbird kept gaining. We were getting to the limit of what Lisa's car would do and it wasn't near enough.

"Take the next road you come to."

"Left, or right?"

"Doesn't matter."

We were going too fast to make the first one, but Lisa had a glimpse of the next one before we got there. She stood on the brakes, threw us into a left-hand skid, and made the turn at thirty. The shoulder strap cut into my ribs. She pushed it to the floor and we roared up a long hill at seventy. The car rattled and the wind whistled through the cracks, but over all the other noise I could clearly hear the engine laboring. The car was giving us all she had.

"He's behind us, but farther back," I said. "Oh, goddam."

"What?"

"There's somebody else behind him. A lot farther back."

"The one from the parking lot?" she asked.

"Maybe. Maybe a third car."

I was still looking back when we crested the hill. "Shit!"

Lisa screamed. I turned around. There was nothing at all in front of us except the night sky. The hill dropped off sharply on the other side and we were airborne. "Jesus!" I yelled.

"Hold her steady!" The time we were in the air couldn't have been long, but it was enough time to sweat. What if we broke something when we hit, or lost control? They'd be on us before we had time for a good prayer.

We crashed heavily onto the road and a metallic thunk reverberated through the car. My ribs screamed in protest as I slammed into the door handle and then into the dashboard.

We bounced into the air again and then down, but not so heavily. Lisa fought the wheel and kept going. Her foot never left the gas. "Feels okay!" she yelled. A groan came from the right front. Neither of us said anything. Either the car would hold together or it wouldn't.

"Up ahead!" she said.

The road went down the hill, curved to the right and went up the next hill. But at the bottom, on the left, were lights. They were too close together for houses, and there were too many for a farm. I could see the dark outline of a large low building. Then I recognized what it was.

"It's a sewage treatment plant," I explained. "If there's an open gate and if you can't see those guys when we get there, kill your lights and turn in."

The plant seemed huge when we reached the bottom of the hill. It was floodlit, and we could see that the gate was open. As we approached, Lisa shut off the lights. I looked back. "Still okay."

Without applying her brakes, she skidded through the gate and drove around the back of the main building. Then she turned around so that we were facing back toward the exit.

"Are we safe now?" she asked.

"For a couple of minutes. They'll go by, sure enough. At least the first one will. But as soon as they realize they've lost us they'll backtrack. How long that will be, I don't know. Depends on the terrain on the other side. If it's open, they'll be starting back in thirty seconds. And this is the only place we could be. They might even send in one of the trailing cars to check this place out now, so we've got to get out of here pretty quick."

"Back the way we came?"

"Yeah, until we can find another road. Look, we need to disguise our lights. You have yellow parking lights in the grill, right?"

"Right."

"Go punch them out, and one of the headlights, too. Take--"She jumped out of the car before I could hand her one of my gloves. Without hesitation, she picked up a rock and slammed it into one parking light, then the other and then the right headlight. Glass crunched on the pavement as she walked back to the car. When she got behind the wheel, blood was running freely down her right hand.

"Jesus, Lisa, you didn't need--" She shook her head impatiently. She was right. There was no point in talking about it. I shut up and watched the road. A pair of headlights belonging to the Thunderbird flashed by, climbing the hill. He must have been doing eighty. His brake lights flashed on and then disappeared over the crest.

There was no one behind him. "Pull out slowly. No lights."

We inched out from the building, feeling naked in the floodlights. No cars in either direction. I cracked my window and listened. Except for the jumble of noises from under our own hood it was quiet. "Turn right, keep it under fifty, turn the lights on when you're completely on the road. I'm going to scrunch down in the seat in case they're counting occupants. Keep me informed."

It hurt like hell to get down on the floor. I could only breathe in shallow pants. We had barely reached the bottom of the hill when she started talking. Her voice was quiet and level "Okay; there's a car coming over the hill toward us. He took a bounce but he's still coming. He's slowing, slowing; now he's past us. He's gone right past the sewer plant and he's going up the next hill. Now he's gone. Now we're back to the big crest; now we're over. Oh, now I can see some more headlights coming up. Jesus, how many cars do these guys have? He's slowing, checking us out, going past. He's behind us now--Damn! He's turning around!" I could feel her accelerating.

"Take the first turn anywhere and punch it." I straightened up; no point in hiding anymore. I looked out the rear window, watching the headlights come around and then point toward us. She found a right and took it as fast as she dared. She was up to forty when we saw farm buildings up ahead.

"Goddam," she yelled. "We're in a farm lane! No way out!"

I looked up. The lane ended just ahead, in a courtyard formed by a house and a couple of barns. I couldn't see any lights. The lane had a drainage ditch down one side. There was only one option left.

"Hit the brakes and stop the car across the lane with my door toward the farm. Then crawl out my side, lie on the ground, and don't move. Try to stay out of sight behind a wheel."

She brought the car to a stop just as I'd asked, across the lane, and I opened the door. Crouching over and trying to ignore the pain, I staggered back toward the roads. I had been thinking of hiding in the drainage ditch, but then I saw a tractor parked near the edge of the field.

Just as I reached the tractor, a pair of headlights turned into the lane. I lay down on the earth on the far side of the tractor. The ground was cold and uneven, and a couple of rocks were jutting into my ribs. The headlights came up fast and stopped about twenty yards to my right. The car must have been pointed in the general direction of the tractor; the headlights brightened everything around me. I was barely hidden behind the front wheels; from where the driver was, my feet were probably visible. I couldn't change position; any motion would make things worse. All I could do was hope that his attention was focused on our car, and that Lisa had followed my instructions.

I closed my eyes and buried my face in the earth, trying to preserve as much of my night vision as I could. I heard a single car door slam. At least he was alone. He left the engine running. Even better. Some sound to mask my noise. Then I heard the unmistakable sound of a pump-action shotgun being worked. As he got closer I heard the crunch of his shoes on the snow. He was walking fast. This was a pro, and one who wasn't going to waste any time.

His steps approached from my right, moved in front of me and then to my left, past my hiding place. I took as deep a breath as my ribs permitted and tried to calm myself. The first shot is your best chance, especially at night. Everyone's vision is ruined by the flashes once the shooting starts. If we were both shooting blindly, a pistol against a shotgun at close range--well, there wasn't much point in dwelling on it. I decided to take the time to cock the .357 and shoot single action. I couldn't afford to let my first shot be anything but my best.

I opened my eyes and extended the gun, bracing my elbows in the earth. Most of the light was off to my right; he and I were both in shadow. In that moment I wasn't dizzy. I didn't have a headache. I wasn't hungry or cold or tired. The only things in my universe were the gun, the target, and my finger on the trigger. I held my gun in my left hand only; using the right for a brace would just punish my ribs more. He was no more than ten yards from me when I cocked my piece.

He was good; he might have sensed my motion as I changed slowly into a firing position, or maybe he saw a glint of moonlight off the barrel as I aimed. He spun around, lowering his shotgun toward my face.

That was as far as he got. Gripping my piece as hard as I could, I gently touched off the first round. The gun bucked in my hand, and the noise rang in my ears like a thunderclap. The bullet hit him like a two-by-four, flinging him backward. The flash from the muzzle dazzled me. Blindly, I followed up with two more shots. I don't know if either of them hit, but after my third shot he staggered and fell to the ground.

As quickly as I could, I got up and shuffled over. I didn't know if he was alive or not. Thinking about what I'd done would have to wait; my concern was keeping myself and Lisa alive. I picked up his shotgun. It was the weapon of a professional. a 12-gauge riot gun with a seven-shot magazine and a folding stock. Putting it on "safe," I hobbled over to his car and turned out the headlights. No point in helping him advertise his location. I glanced around the car; it was equipped with both a cellular phone and a CB. If we were lucky we had a minute and a half to get the hell out of there.

One hand bloody, Lisa helped me into the passenger seat. "Let's get out of here. If he told them where he was going, the others will be here when he doesn't report back."

"What about him?"

"They'll be here soon enough. They'll take care of him. One way or another."

She made a right onto the main road, then took the next right. This one was a road, not a lane, and we followed it several miles. Behind us, it stayed dark and silent. Finally, the road brought us out in a little town named Cambridge. We stopped behind a building for ten minutes. No cars went past.

"So far so good," I said.

"Until tomorrow."

"We'll worry about that tomorrow. For now, follow this road. It should run into Gault Road. That'll take us right where we want to go."

"How can you know all these roads?"

"I stay with my friend weekends in the summer. We ride bikes all around here. When you're moving at ten miles an hour there's plenty of time to consider the roads." Bicycling. On a warm summer's day. It was hard to remember, at that moment, what that was like.

We reached the base of a line of ridges and started up. We were in the Welsh Mountains. The farmhouses stopped once we started climbing, and the bare fields were replaced by stands of scrub pine. I looked back the entire time; there was nothing behind us. After we'd climbed steadily for a few minutes, I told her to slow down. "Turn off your headlights and just creep along for a bit. If there's anyone trailing us we haven't seen, this'll flush them out."

"How could that be, if we can't see them?"

"Infrared. Not very likely, but possible. We have to be careful. If we lead them to the cabin, there's nowhere else we can go."

We went a few hundred yards with no lights, edging off onto the shoulder a couple of times, till I was satisfied.

"Okay, the road is going to dip down. At the bottom of the dip is a trail to the right. Take it without using your brakes and pull up so there are trees on both sides."

It was an inelegant turn, but at least she did it without activating the brake lights. And the trail sloped upwards, so we came to a halt without needing them for that. After the last half hour, being still was an unfamiliar feeling. We watched and listened for several minutes.

"We're alone," I said at last. "We lost them."

"For sure?"

"Sure as I can be." She put her head back against the headrest and closed her eyes. I wanted to ask her what she was thinking, then decided not to. "All right," I continued. "You can use your lights now. Up the trail a bit is a chain across the road. It has a padlock with a combination, 440. Lock it up again behind us and drive up to the cabin."

After the gate, the trail went into a climbing turn and leveled off at the cabin, in a clearing at the top of the hill. It was a modern log construction with a stone chimney, surrounded by a split-rail fence. I got the key from under the porch. Inside, except for the bedroom and bathroom in the interior, was one big room, with broad-plank yellow pine floors. "This is great," Lisa said. "Does your friend come here often?"

"In the summer he and his wife come up for the weekends. I think he has a girlfriend and they use it during the week, sometimes. Nobody uses it in the winter at all."

I set down my pistol and pumped the shotgun to eject the shell. Lisa picked it up and looked at it carefully. "Doesn't look like much. Not like a bullet, I mean. It's mostly red plastic. Looks like a firecracker."

I took it from her and held it between two fingers. "It's double-aught buckshot. A second later and my mother couldn't have identified me."

I put the round back into the magazine with the others and put on the safety. I turned away, so she wouldn't see how hard my hands were shaking. Lisa looked up at the cathedral ceiling. "After twenty-four hours of being chased and terrorized I had forgotten what it was like to feel safe again."

"We're as safe as we can be till this is over."

"Let's think about now."

I cranked up the heat--it was left at fifty anyway to keep the pipes from freezing--and looked through the cupboards and found some cans of spaghetti. It was all we had other than a jar of black olives. Lisa brought in some wood and went to work kindling a fire in the massive stone fireplace that took up most of one wall. By the time I'd finished my food inventory, she was sitting on her haunches on a fake bearskin rug in front of a blazing fire.

"You do good work," I said.

"When you heat with wood you get a lot of practice."

"Come in the bathroom and let me look at your hand."

I rolled up her sleeve to the elbow and let her hand soak in lukewarm water. The knuckles and the back of her hand were a mess. Small cuts crisscrossed at different angles, and there were four deep lacerations starting just behind the knuckles; two of them halfway to the wrist, and all of them were deep even to show flaps of loose skin.

"You're going to have to do the work," she said. "I can't do this left-handed."

"Can you move the fingers? If you can't then you have to see a doctor for tendon repairs."

"They move fine." When I stopped running the water, the deep cuts were still bleeding a little, and embedded glass glittered in the harsh bathroom light. "Let me get you a drink."

"I'll be okay. Just get to work."

"It's going to hurt."

"I'm used to pain."

There were no tweezers in the medicine cabinet, but she'd brought a pair in her bag. I worked with my right hand despite the pain it caused my side; there was no other way. Extracting the glass was slow work and concentrating gave me a headache. Some pieces were round and easy to see. Others were slivers that only showed when the light hit a certain way. Every time I pulled a piece out it caused fresh bleeding. I would work on one laceration for a while and then move to another till the bleeding in the first one subsided enough for me to see what I was doing. I was no doctor, and I'm sure I was clumsy as hell, but she never moved a muscle.

"Okay," I said. I picked up a bottle of hydrogen peroxide, the only disinfectant we had. "This is going to hurt." She nodded. I poured the bottle liberally all over her hand. The peroxide foamed and bubbled everywhere it touched raw flesh. Even though it didn't matter anymore, she kept her hand perfectly still.

When the bubbling subsided, I wrapped her hand in a thin hand towel and taped it into a rough bandage. "I'll change it again in the morning. I got what I could, but you'd better see a doctor when this is over."

"I could use that drink now."

I rummaged in the medicine cabinet. My friend was half-way to a hypochondriac, and I found what I was looking for. "Look, here are some sleeping pills. "Take something before you hit the hay. That thing's going to throb. You might as well try and sleep through it."

I found a couple of bottles of champagne in the refrigerator, left over from Lord knows what tryst or family occasion, and filled jelly jars for us. "Take it easy for a few minutes. I'm going to take a shower. Then you can take one and we can have some dinner."

My clothes were in a sad state. They weren't clean when I'd put them on this morning and the events of the day hadn't helped. Everything was filthy. My shirt was blotchy pink from diluted bloodstains, three of the buttons were missing, and the right sleeve was half torn off at the shoulder. Somehow, at some point, I'd ripped one knee out of my pants. Even my undershirt was torn.

I put on one of the bathrobes hanging behind the bathroom door and hung my clothes up to dry. There was no razor. I would just have to let my beard go for another day.

While Lisa took her shower I assembled our dinner, which mostly involved opening a can and heating the spaghetti in the microwave. She came back wearing the other bathrobe. Her hair was wet, and she let it loose to dry. I hadn't seen her with her hair down before. I couldn't decide if it made her look younger, or just different. Either way, despite everything, including her bandaged hand, she was lovely. We ate sitting on the bearskin next to the fire. She ate without looking at her food. Not much was said. It had been a terrible twenty-four hours and both of us were simply glad to be alive. Talking about it wasn't necessary. We had been through it together. And as equals. Whatever distance there was between us as professional and client went away the moment she stepped into her kitchen the night before. I owed her far more than she owed me. No, it was past being about owing.

When we were finished I threw another log on the fire while she cleared away the plates. She turned off the lights, came back with some pillows, and put them behind me. Then she shrugged off her bathrobe, lay down beside me, and pulled the robe over both of us.

"What are we going to do tomorrow?" she asked.

"We're safe if we don't do anything but just go to the hearing. They don't know where we are now, so if we take a back way to Philly, they're not going to find us. Once we get to the courthouse there's no problem. There's security and metal detectors and cops everywhere."

"What about afterwards?"

"We'll think about that afterwards."

She used her left hand to open my robe and rub my chest.

"It's all been like a dream," she said softly. "In a way, everything since Dan died has. But the last two days especially. If I didn't hurt so much I wouldn't be sure it was really happening."

"It is, believe me."

"What are you thinking?" she asked.

"About the man in the farm lane."

"You shouldn't think about that."

"No, you're right," I said. I was looking at the ceiling. At that moment Lisa seemed far away and the man in the lane seemed very close. "It doesn't do any good. But this is new for me. I mean, I know guns because I need to know my job. But I've never killed anything. Before this, I mean. Even in the war. I don't even hunt."

"He could have been the one that killed Dan."

"If it wasn't him, it might as well have been." Neither of us said anything for a while. "You know the worst part of killing him?"

"Stop it. You had to do it."

"The worst part isn't that he's dead; he probably deserved worse. It's that I know that I can kill, when I'm not in a war. I don't like knowing that about myself."

"That's what I learned last night with those bikers, so I guess we're even."

"Let's not talk anymore."

She put her cheek against my shoulder and kissed me gently on the neck. I kissed her back, a long time, and put my arm around her. With my right hand I traced the line of her jaw. She closed her eyes and pressed her cheek against my palm. Then her left hand slid down my chest and untied the knot in my robe.

Her fingers moved down my stomach to my groin. We were ready for each other. She threw a leg over me and guided me inside. As she straightened up, straddling me, her robe fell away from her shoulders. When she threw it clear, her hair shadowed her face. She pulled it back, tying it into a rough knot. "I don't want it getting in the way." As she tied it, I watched the line of her body from her arm running down her side, narrowing at the waist and flaring out a little at the hip. It was the way I'd thought she would look, smooth and graceful and athletic. Very gently, I ran one finger all the way from her shoulder to her knee, getting to know her.

The firelight outlined her body in flickering reds and golds. I ran my hands over her thighs, up her sides, and over her breasts. "You are beautiful," I said slowly.

She looked away. "I'm glad you think so."

"More than beautiful. Exquisite."

"Now you're teasing."

"Absolutely not. "I put a hand on each side of her waist.

"Of all the places in the world I could be right now, I can't think of one I'd rather be than right here."

She laughed. "My God, you must be Irish."

"Hardly. Russian Jew. And a very secular one at that."

She began moving her hips slowly back and forth, then more urgently. "As much," she gasped, "as I'd like to continue this conversation, it feels too good to wait. Don't worry about me. This one's for you. "There was no finesse in the way she rode me the first time; it was quick and sweaty and a little rough. When she sensed I was ready to come she started contracting herself around me till she milked dry. After we finished she stayed astride me, watching for what seemed like a long time. Her face was completely serious. "Was it okay?"

"Now you're the one who's teasing."

"I really want to know." Her voice was serious.

I brought her face down to me and kissed her. Some loose strands of hair fell in my face. "You've got a lot of nerve asking that. It was wonderful."

"Really?"

"Really."

I could feel the tension flowing out of her body. "I'm glad."

I thought of the vibrator and the unopened box of condoms in her dresser. "I feel badly now, about going through your personal things."

"You pick a funny time to get embarrassed. "She slid off me and moved down to my crotch. "I hope you're not too shy for this?"

"I'll have to think about that for a tenth of a second. Okay, then. All right, I suppose. Jesus Christ, what are--how did you learn to do that?"

I was forty-four years old, my side hurt, I had a headache that felt like the end of the world, and I'd drunk more champagne than was good for me. None of that mattered. In a few minutes she was back on top and we were making love again.

The second time was hers. With my ribs I couldn't move much, but she didn't mind; she set the pace. She was in no hurry to finish and neither was I. As far as I was concerned, it could have gone on forever.

CHAPTER TWELVE
Monday, 5:00 A.M.

The fire was dying down when I awoke. For a few minutes I lay there watching the play of the firelight on the ceiling. Lisa was burrowed against my side, her leg thrown over mine and her breasts pressed against my ribs on my good side. The firelight played on the curves of her body. Her breathing was deep and regular, and she was snoring, just a little. Her hair, next to my nose, smelled of sex and pine smoke and shampoo.

I wanted to turn but that was not possible without either disturbing Lisa or rolling onto my damaged side, so I stayed still. In addition to my ribs and my headache, I had a new discomfort, this one in my rear. The second time, after Lisa was too exhausted to continue, she decided to help me over the top with a finger against my prostate. I shifted to keep the sore spot off the bearskin.

I tried to go back to sleep and failed. I started thinking about Lisa and pressed my lips gently against her hair. But that was a luxury. There was a case and it wasn't finished. I stared at the ceiling and tried to put the pieces together. I studied the knotholes in the ceiling, watching the play of the firelight. The holes were scattered randomly, here were three small ones close together forming a triangle, over there was a pair, and directly above me, one large one in isolation. There was no pattern. The more I tried to impose one the more disjointed it seemed.

What is thinking, really? How can you explain how it is that you come to understand something? You try to teach a child that two and two are four; he looks at you blankly at first, and then his face lights up and he gets it. But there's nothing in between—either the connection is made, or it isn't.

That was what happened to me in the quiet hour before dawn. One moment the case was as obscure as ever; the next moment I had the solution. It wasn't a question of making the knotholes do what I wanted; it was seeing what had always been there. The only reason it had been hard to see was because I'd refused to see it. I didn't feel elated. I just felt like an idiot. The solution had been starting me in the face all along. I had finally seen what was in front of my nose.

"Lisa," I whispered. "Lisa, honey, we need to get up."

Initially there was no response. Either she was a very sound sleeper or the combination of champagne and sleeping pills had hit her pretty hard. I flattered myself that the sex had something to do with it, too.

"Lisa," I said, louder. "We have to go."

Her face appeared, her eyes half open. "Huh?"

"We need to get to Philadelphia."

"It's the middle of the night."

"It's going to be dawn in an hour. We have things to do. Now."

"Let's do this some more. Or sleep "

"Later. There'll be plenty of time for that later. But we need to go now. It's important."

"Those pills. Arghh." But she was awake, at least a little. I was so tired I could barely move, but I managed to get her leg off me and stand up. The room danced around, but not as badly as yesterday.

My headache had receded to the point where I could work around it. I dressed while Lisa struggled to wake up. Then I changed her bandage and checked outside while she dressed. It was still dark, but as far as I could tell, there were no footprints except for our own. The engine hadn't been tampered with. I felt as safe as I could expect to. I put the shotgun in the back seat under a blanket and the pistol back in my pocket. Lisa shuffled onto the porch, rubbing her eyes. Despite the cold her jacket was unbuttoned. Her feet were barely moving.

"Want me to drive?" she offered gamely.

"Thanks. I'm better today. And you're still sleepy. If you'll just do the gate for me on the way out that'll be fine. Then you can go back to sleep."

She took me up on it; by the time we reached Route 897 and headed toward the turnpike, she was out. I was fine with that. It was going to be a big day and at least one of us needed to be rested. I drove with one hand on her thigh and felt her warmth.

It was just after six, and still dark, when I pulled into the Valley Forge rest stop and found a phone booth with a directory. I put in my quarters and a sleepy male voice answered.

"Hello?"

"Leo Strasnick?"

"Yes. Who is this? Do you know what time it is?"

"This is Dave Garrett, Mr. Strasnick. And it's time to die."

The line was silent for the space of half a dozen heartbeats. "What are you talking about? And who are you? Aren't you--"

"You know exactly what I mean and who I am. And you have one slim chance to save your miserable ass. Meet me in the parking lot of the King of Prussia shopping center in half an hour. Don't be late and be sure you come alone."

"I can't get there that fast."

"If you hurry you can." I couldn't afford to give him any time to organize himself.

"It's a huge lot. What if I miss you?"

"Then you'll be dead. But out of deference to your lifestyle, we'll meet at the main entrance to Bloomingdale's." I hung up.

Lisa was still sleeping, so I got a big coffee and sat with her, keeping the engine running so she'd be warm. I twisted the wrong way buckling my seat belt, and my ribs renewed their complaint. The coffee brought back the pounding in the back of my head, but at least I was fully awake. I would need my wits today I was hurting and exhausted and the worst was still ahead.

I finished my coffee and drove the ten minutes to the mall. Although the sky was starting to lighten in the east, it was still dark. I parked in the middle of the vast parking lot, about a hundred yards from the Bloomingdale's entrance, with the car pointed toward the exit. The lot was well illuminated, and there were no other cars in sight.

"Lisa, wake up. It's time."

She breathed heavily once and opened her eyes.

She looked around and took a deep breath. "I'm getting tired of asking this, but what's the plan? It's too early to shop."

"I'm going to meet with Leo Strasnick in a minute. You have to be backup."

That woke her up. "Strasnick? Danny's old partner? What for?"

"There isn't time to explain now. Just take it for granted he's dangerous. I handed her the shotgun.

"When he parks, roll your window down and sit with the gun sitting up so he can see it. Don't point it; just let him see you have it. Have you ever fired a pump shotgun before?"

"Just that .22 pistol."

"It's easy enough to use. Right now, it's safe. If there's trouble, put your hand here on the slide and pump it back once, as hard as you can, then forward again. That will carry a shell from the magazine into the chamber. Then press this button here behind the trigger to the left so that the red is showing. See that?"

"Yeah." She wasn't crazy about this part of the plan.

"That button is the safety; when you can see the red, the safety is off, and you can fire. With me so far?"

"Got it."

"Point it at his car and put the stock back hard against your shoulder. Then pull the trigger. It'll kick, so hold on tight. You reload by working the slide again, to feed another round. There are seven shots. When you're finished, hide the gun under the blanket and get the hell back to North Carbon. If you go by a river or a lake, throw the thing in."

"What about you?"

"When I said if there was trouble, I meant that I would be dead already. If you do your job, Strasnick will be, too."

"Why would he want to hurt you?"

"He may not. I just want to make sure he won't try."

"Do you have to do this?"

"It's this or spend the rest of our lives like we spent the last two days."

A black Mercedes sedan with tinted windows pulled into the parking lot, roared past us, and stopped about a hundred yards away. I opened my door and stood with the door between me and him. I motioned for him to come closer. Then I motioned him to my right, on the passenger side, so Lisa could have a clear shot. When he was close, I nodded, and his engine died.

I swallowed and walked towards his car. The only sound was my steps on the concrete. I tried not to think that at any moment one of those black windows could roll down and leave me staring down the muzzle of a gun. I also didn't like the idea of the tinted windows; Lisa wouldn't be able to see anything until it was too late.

I walked slowly around to the passenger's side and opened the door. Strasnick was there, his hair tousled, wearing a navy blazer with no tie. His hands were on the wheel and he was alone.

"Strasnick, before I get in, I set the ground rules. See the woman in my car? See the gun? It's a police riot gun, and if anything funny happens it'll shred your tires, your sheet metal, your glass, and you, too. Play it straight."

I got in and shut the door.

"I have no intention of harming you or anyone else, Mr. Garrett. And I don't like threats. As a matter of fact, I don't know why I didn't just call the police and report--"

I hit him with a short right jab. It was awkwardly thrown, but I put as much into it as I could; his head snapped back and banged into the driver's side window with a satisfying noise. When he recovered, he was bleeding from the corner of his mouth. My side burned like hell, but it was worth it, for a lot of reasons.

"That's for trying to bullshit me. I've come too far to fuck around. 'You know where that riot gun comes from? Your man that didn't come back last night? I killed him and I took it away from him."

"My man? What are you talking about?"

"Okay. You shut up and I'll explain it to you." My headache was reaching new heights, so strong I could barely concentrate, and throwing the punch hadn't done my ribs and good. Then I thought of Lisa and her hand and stopped feeling sorry for myself.

"Wilson was tired of working for the mob. I don't know if he was scared, or fed up, or what, but he didn't need the money badly enough to keep on doing it. But you did. He was an unhappy guy for lots of reasons, you're right about that. But he really did want out of the partnership—because you weren't willing to change. You kept bringing him those cases and he had to take them as long as he was in the firm."

I wanted to rub my temples, but I didn't want to let him see it. "And then the fifty thousand came in; it must have looked pretty good to you. Back in those days, tax-free, it was a year's income, or more. When the client died, you took it and hoped you'd never hear about it. Wilson wanted no part of it; he said you were crazy. Am I right?"

Strasnick didn't scare easy. "Only a little. You're very badly misinformed. I've nothing to hide. Dan's representatives are free to check the accounts. There was a large fee, as you said, just before he disappeared. The client deposited a substantial retainer and then died. Dan declined his share—he said I was entitled to the whole thing for bringing the client. And a share of that money was spent on upgrading the office, from which we all benefited, by the way. That's all there is to say. Mr. Garrett, for a former practitioner, you have some very simpleminded ideas about a law practice."

"I have some simpleminded ideas about how the books can be cooked. So, it wasn't tax-free—no difference. You made up a receipt for the money, ran it through the firm as income to avoid the IRS getting on your ass, and kept it yourself. It squared you with the feds, but it didn't help you with the people who really mattered. They found out somehow that their man had left the money with your firm, and they asked for it back. And that's when you made your move. You decided to ingratiate yourself with them and get rid of your partner at the same time. You told them he took it."

"That's preposterous. There's not a shred of evidence that it happened that way."

"Don't talk to me about evidence. They know what you told them. That's why they tried to kill Dan. And they know how you lied to them about me and this case."

"What are you talking about?"

A minor leap. "You told someone I know that I was looking for Wilson's killers, which I wasn't. You knew perfectly well I was just establishing that the man hadn't been heard from in seven years; I wasn't looking for anything else. Why lie, unless you were afraid of what I'd find? And why send the muscle out to Lisa Wilson's house?"

"What?"

"I thought they were from the organization, but I was wrong. You have some connections of your own. You must still do plenty of mob work; it's just that now you've upgraded to a better class of referrals. Helping to arrange buyouts of legit businesses, infiltrate unions, launder money, things like that. You know names of your own now. You called those boys out to North Carbon yourself.

"I'm guessing that you just wanted them to trash the house; maybe that would scare Lisa off. And that it was pure bad luck they showed up when someone was home. But with the story you gave them, they would have killed me trying to get money that didn't exist in the first place. And you called out the ones who were after us last night, too. Again, why? Because you have something to hide. Who else could have known to call out the boys to the scene of the shooting Friday night? And who scared off the Shreiner Agency?

"Who else could have known to call Brogan and scare him off? Don't try to kid me. You were partners with Wilson for years; you had to know the name of his closest friend. The only reason you didn't scare off his old girlfriend is because you couldn't find her. She'd married and changed her name and moved away."

"I assume you can prove all this."

"Not in court, but that doesn't matter."

"I beg your pardon?"

"You should, for trying to kill me at least twice. I can prove it with a phone call to my contact. He'll know those men weren't following orders from him. He'll make a couple of phone calls and he'll know that they took on a job for you."

"That still doesn't connect me with anything they would really care about. If I had the connections to call out people on my own, then why should they care?"

"It's not just that you use them, but what you use them for. In this case, it shows you were covering up your theft."

"And what evidence is there of that, except your own speculations years after the fact?"

"Daniel Wilson."

"He's been dead for years. Don't play games with me."

I leaned close and locked eyes with him. "He's very much alive."

"I don't believe it."

"You'd better. If you don't, and he comes forward and tells his story, you'll be in the kind of trouble no one comes back from. You stole from them, you lied to them about who did it, and you sent out one of their men on a cover-up errand that got him killed."

"Are you trying to threaten me with criminal charges?"

"I'm not going to fool around with that. All I have to do is call one of these numbers." I handed him the business card, now creased and grimy, with the telephone numbers.

He looked at the card for a long time, a lot longer than it took to understand what it meant. He swallowed, and his hand shook. He handed the card back as if trying to force the genie back in the bottle.

"What do you want?"

"One hundred twenty thousand dollars."

"You're insane!"

"No, I'm just not finished. What I gave you was just what you need to do this morning. Within the next couple of days your firm is going to vote to pay off the Wilson estate its one hundred thousand for Wilson's share of the partnership--without the insurance money."

"This—this--" He sat there with his mouth open, trying to absorb it all. "How can I possibly--"

"Put the squeeze on your banker for a fast home equity loan, clean out your accounts, get a cash advance on your bankcard, call your friends, sell your stock, and go to the loan sharks for the rest. Whatever else you say about those people, they work fast. It's amazing what can be done when there's no paperwork."

"But they'll charge me a point a day! There's no way I could ever repay--"

I was getting tired of his whining. I pulled out the magnum and placed the muzzle on the bridge of his nose. "Now pay attention, because I'm only going to say this once. If you don't have the money by noon, I call my contact and tell him what I know. You're dead by evening and probably your family, too. The family part is out of my hands. The first hundred thousand is going to the mob to repay what you stole in the first place. I hate doing this, but I can't buy peace for one of you without doing it for both. Personally I'd prefer to see you dead. You may wind up that way anyway; if you don't repay the loan sharks you know what happens. But I'm giving you more of a chance than you ever gave Dan."

"You can't be so arbitrary! You have to give me some time to work this--" I leaned close to his face. "Strasnick, listen up. I had a friend who was an assistant DA. One night the Philly police called him to the scene of where the mob had been questioning one of their people about a theft, just like this one. They'd taken him out to his garage, parked his car on top of his hands, and used his own lawn mower on him. From the cigarette butts, it looked like they'd been there a long time. If you want to go that way, it's fine with me."

He started to sob--strange, choking sounds unlike any human noise I'd ever heard. I put the gun away.

"I want the money in cash—large bills—in a briefcase. It must be ready at noon. The meeting place will be in Center City. I'll call your office later this morning when I know where."

His sobbing continued. "Look, tell me right now. Can you do it by noon or should I just go ahead and make the call?"

"No--I can do it."

He was looking down, his mouth slightly open, looking at something a hundred miles in the ground.

"And one more thing," I said. He didn't look up. "You made quite a speech two days ago about what it means to be partners. Tell me just how you got around to fingering him. I want to know."

He looked at me mildly. His voice was barely above a whisper.

"Does it matter now?"

"It matters to me."

"For years we'd busted our asses. Working fourteen-hour days, kissing ass with clients. I hardly ever saw my kids and we were still broke. Then they came along. We had it made. Until Dan lost his nerve."

"Couldn't you just go on without him?"

"With any other client, sure. But if he walked, they'd never trust us again. They're not very trusting people. They don't accept excuses. The day he left was the last day we'd have all those clients. I had the other lawyers to think of, and my family . . . " He looked into my eyes and trailed off.

I got out. I spent a couple of minutes back in Lisa's car, putting the shotgun back on safe, hiding it, and generally pulling myself together. She didn't speak. When we drove away, the Mercedes still hadn't moved.

CHAPTER THIRTEEN
Monday, 8:00 A.M.

As I headed toward Philadelphia, the eastern sky was streaked with pink and rose. In my mood it reminded me of blood, but I kept that to myself. We were still too early for the start of the rush hour, but traffic was heavy.

"Lisa, there aren't any assets in Dan's estate other than the insurance policy, are there?"

She'd shaken off the hangover from the sleeping pills. "No. Nothing. Why do you ask?"

"I have a proposition for you. If I could get you the insurance money without going through with the hearing, would you be willing to drop the case?"

"Of course. But how can you do that?"

"Do you need to check with your mom?"

"She wants nothing to do with this. She signed it over to me if we get it. She thinks it's blood money. She may be right."

"I've got a plan. It's still tentative. First I've got some calls to make."

'What kind of plan?"

"I've got to finish working this out. We'll talk more later. Trust me on this for a couple hours, okay?"

"I trust you."

When we crawled as far as City Line Avenue I got off and found a pay phone. First, I called Mark Louchs.

'Hello?" From the sound of his voice I'd woken him up. That made me feel better. "Mark, this is Dave."

"Oh! Great. I was wondering what the hell happened. When I hire an investigator, I expect him to keep in closer contact—"

Asshole, I thought to myself. "That's a long story. Look, I think the case is going to fold up."

"That's what lawyers tell investigators, not the other way around." He couldn't help rubbing it in.

"A lot has happened and there's more to come."

'What are you talking about?"

"I can't say right now. Just take that on faith, okay?"

"Did they get to you, too?"

"It's nothing like that, believe me. Just take it on faith."

"This sounds like it's out of control."

"Not entirely. Just work with me for a couple of hours."

"If you say so."

"I do. But I can't say more now. Things are in a state of flux. I'll know more soon. Listen, you have this case on an hourly rate or contingent?"

"Hourly."

"Would four thousand cover your time and expenses to date?"

"Shreiner returned us what we'd paid them, so yes, I think so. Except for your time."

"If I can make this deal fly, I'll be in a position to guarantee your fee." It was an easy promise to make. If I didn't, I'd be at the bottom of Tinnicum Marsh.

"Fine, thank you. But what's going on?"

"I'll fill you in later." It was the first flat out lie I'd told him. "Have to go now. 'Bye."

Next, I called the bottom number on the card the attorney had given me.

"Yeah?" a male voice answered. Not polite or rude, just neutral.

'This is Dave Garrett. I was told I could reach the counselor at this number."

I was put on hold. The line produced a series of clicks, buzzes, and intermittent tones. Once, it sounded completely dead and I was afraid I'd been disconnected. But then his voice, unmistakable, came on the line. It was full and clear, and it felt as if he were in the booth with me. I didn't like it.

"Good morning, Garrett. You're an early riser."

"There have been some developments. I have a proposal that I think you'll like."

"Business should be done face-to-face."

"That's why I'm calling."

"Where are you now?"

"At the City Line exit off the Schuylkill. In a phone booth."

"Perhaps you are. Wait in your car at your office." The connection was broken.

We headed south on City Line and stopped at a fast-food joint for breakfast. I didn't notice the name of the franchise or what we ordered, but I recall going into the washroom and looking in the mirror. I looked like a panhandler who'd lost a fight over a bottle of Mad Dog. My face was dirty and unshaven, my hair was a mess, and the bruises were ripening to a sickly olive-yellow.

Lisa had been patient about waiting for answers, more patient than I would have been. She could see I was at the end of my rope and she was doing what she could to make it easy on me. Now I had a moment for some explanation.

"We're dealing with the big boys. We edged out their second string. And even their first string, once. But our luck is going to run out. We have to end this. The only way to do that is to talk to them. If I can't sell my idea I'm in trouble. If you're with me, you're in trouble, too. Up to now you've just been someone who's with me. They have no reason to get you. To keep it that way you have to stay clear for a little while."

"We're in this together."

"Nice thought, but there's nothing you can do to help.

All you can do is endanger yourself. So stay out."

"Why did you want to talk to Strasnick?" she asked.

"Even telling you would endanger you. And there isn't time to get into it, anyway. Just take it easy."

"Take it easy? What are you saying?"

"I have to do a meeting. I know what I want to do, and I think it will go well. When it's done, we'll have all the time in the world to talk. I'm not going anywhere. I want you to understand that. Because I have to ask you to just trust me some more."

She put her hand on mine and I had my answer.

We ate quickly and headed out. I stopped in front of a branch of the public library about a half mile from my office. I kept my eyes open; no one was following us. "Just go in there and sit tight. I'll be back in an hour or two." If I'm back at all.

"David, please take good care of yourself,"

"I haven't done very well so far, have I?"

'You're still alive," she said. "I want you to stay that way."

"I'm alive because of you. I need to do this for your sake and mine."

"I think my mother is right, this is blood money. Last night—"

"Last night meant a lot to me, too. But talking about it is going to have to wait. Now get inside before somebody sees you."

She kissed me on the lips, hard, and I kissed her back. For a moment she pressed her cheek against mine. Then she got out of the car. As she walked away, I saw that her bandage was bloody again. It gave me a sick feeling, half a fear and half a memory. I thought how easy it would be for someone to let all her life out, not just that little bit of blood, right there on the sidewalk. All they needed was a clean shot and a getaway car. And if I failed it could come to that.

I drove to my office and parked out front. Fortunately for my nerves I didn't have long to wait. Within ten minutes a car with two men I hadn't seen before pulled up. The one in the back motioned for me to get in. The search was conducted in silence. Then we got on Roosevelt Boulevard and headed north. We took an exit in Northeast Philadelphia, cut through a shopping center and stopped in front of a brick bungalow in a residential area. The driver escorted me to the door. The other man followed us at a safe distance and then headed around to the rear.

The house was barren of any furnishings, and unheated. I could see my breath in the air. As soon as I shut the door behind me,

I heard footsteps upstairs, on the stairway. The sound echoed through the bare rooms.

The lawyer came down the stairs, wearing a black hat, yellow silk scarf, and a black cashmere overcoat. He was fresh and rested, and despite his years there was a bounce in his step. Leaning against the door for support, I felt like his grandfather.

"Mr. Garrett." He squinted slightly when my face moved into the light. 'What happened?"

"Occupational injuries. From Saturday night."

He nodded slowly. "Saturday night. Accidental?"

"No."

"My client wasn't involved." It was a statement of fact, not just a reassurance. This man knew every detail.

"If they were, it wasn't a matter of policy, I'm sure."

"Please come into the kitchen. We have a table and some chairs. It's a crude arrangement, but this is short notice."

We sat down across from each other with our coats on, our breath visible in the air. I liked the cold; it kept me from sweating with fear so much.

He studied me before he spoke. "You said you had a proposal?"

I moistened my lips and spoke slowly. I couldn't lie, and I couldn't give anything away that I didn't have to. "Seven years ago, fifty thousand dollars in cash disappeared. A misunderstanding arose as to the identity of the person responsible. What my clients need now is . . . let me choose the right word. Amnesty."

He spoke abruptly. "Wilson wasn't responsible?"

"It was more complex than you were led to believe."

"Answer my question."

There was no point in being indirect. I wasn't going to play games to cover Strasnick. "You were given bad information."

"How can you be sure?"

"One of my clients told me so."

"Who exactly?"

"I can't say without breaching multiple confidences and blowing up the agreement."

"Please." It wasn't a request.

I temporized. "Once you hear me out, you'll see what I mean."

He sighed impatiently. "All right."

"In exchange for amnesty my clients are prepared to not only replace the missing property, but to double it. And as a token of their sincerity, they will pay one hundred thousand. The payment will be ready at noon today. The hearing scheduled for today in the Wilson disappearance will be canceled and the case will be withdrawn permanently. You will never hear the name Daniel Wilson again."

"So Wilson is alive, somehow."

I swallowed. The thought of trying to lie to this man terrified me. "The bullets didn't kill him."

He made an angry gesture at the ceiling, directed at whatever men he had upstairs. For the first time there was real emotion in his voice. "These men today--cars, bombs, rifles, even! Long range, indirect. They want distance. They don't want to look their man in the eye. The old ways were the best. You knew the job was done. You had to come to grips, you understand? They don't like that anymore. With the old ways there were no mistakes."

I could have talked about mistakes. Instead I just waited.

"Where is he?"

I swallowed. "I can't say."

"Where?"

I maintained eye contact and slowly shook my head. "I came here trusting that we could speak in good faith. You told me Saturday that I had your authority to recover the money. I've done that for you, and more. All without any publicity and at no cost to you. If we have a deal, then you don't need to know. Our deal was the return of the property. Not information."

He held my eyes while he appraised me. Or rather, while he decided whether it was worth the trouble to find out. It took no more than a few seconds, but in that time, I saw what some dead men have seen. He didn't care if he killed me or not, if it advanced the interests of his client. In the house were men who could work me over this morning, kill me in the afternoon and forget it by dinner; and if he said the word, I was theirs.

He considered me. Then, very slowly, he relaxed, and his eyes clouded over again. He leaned back in the chair.

"We know what we need to know." He seemed to be talking to himself, his mind on something else. "The property would be in what form?"

"Cash, large bills, in a briefcase."

"And who exactly are you representing? Exactly who is getting forgiveness?" His voice was bored; he knew the answer already.

The rules of confidentiality didn't make much sense under the circumstances. "One of the parties you know already; the Wilson family. The other's identity--well, there's no point in trying to keep it a secret--is Leo Strasnick."

"I'm a bit surprised that Mr. Strasnick feels he needs his own representation and that he feels that his interests are in accord with those of the Wilson family."

"He decided that just this morning, as a matter of fact."

He found that amusing, in his fashion. "We may have to reevaluate the utility of a continuing relationship with attorney Strasnick."

"What happens in the future is up to you, as long as we have a deal about the past."

"Amnesty." He said it slowly, mulling over the word on his tongue.

"For both." It stuck in my throat, but I got it out.

He sighed. "Mr. Garrett, your terms are acceptable. My people will pick you up at a place of your choosing in the downtown area with the money at noon. They will take you to a neutral location for the count and then drop you where you wish. Where shall I have them pick you up?"

"Corner of Sixteenth and Market." Strasnick's building. "That concludes our present business." His voice took on a different note, no warmer, but less formal. "Mr. Garrett, you handle yourself well. Have you had a chance to consider my offer about reinstatement?"

"Thank you. But the answer is still no." I thought about the best way of phrasing it. "It would be a debt I would have trouble repaying."

He nodded. "The count will be handled by one of my assistants. We will not be meeting again. And I would trouble you for the return of my card."

He extended his hand and I passed it to him. I was happy to be rid of it. The room was cold, but his hand was colder. I hoped I would never have to touch or even see that man again.

Within thirty minutes I was back at the library. She was sitting in the entryway nursing a cup of coffee. When she looked up, she looked behind me to see if I was alone.

"How are we doing?"

"Everything's fine. We shook hands on the deal. It will all be over by noon."

"Can you tell me what's going on now? I feel I'm going to explode." She was exasperated, and I couldn't blame her.

"If there's a problem at the other end, with Strasnick, there could still be trouble. I can't say any more than that. Come on."

We got into her car and headed south, with no destination in mind. I was more concerned than I let on to Lisa. I had to kill two hours and I felt safer on the move in a big city than in a fixed location. Not that I was expecting any trouble, but I'd already had a bellyful of the unexpected kind.

"Lisa, we need to have a talk."

"We sure do. The—"

"We need to talk about the past before we talk about the present."

"What about the past?"

"This all started seven years ago with fifty thousand in cash that belonged to the mob. Strasnick took it and blamed it on Dan. That's why they were after him. That's what Strasnick and I talked about in the car. He's going to replace the money, double it as a matter of fact."

"Strasnick?"

"He knew I could prove that he'd been after me, but he really didn't care about that. His friends in the organization wouldn't care if he had a grudge against an outsider, if that was all there was to it. He was only worried about the money being traced back to him.

He didn't believe I had any proof about what happened seven years ago."

She said nothing.

"What do you think I told him?"

"I don't know."

"Yes, you do."

Silence.

I did something I'd never done, either as a lawyer or investigator: I begged a witness. "Lisa don't make me do this. I'd like you to tell me yourself."

Silence. I was busy driving and couldn't look at her.

"Lisa, I told him Daniel Wilson is alive."

I pulled over and parked.

CHAPTER FOURTEEN
Monday, 10:00 A.M.

She looked out the window a long time without speaking. If I didn't know her, and what the question meant, I might have thought she hadn't heard. I caught a glimpse of the side of her face. I can't describe what I saw, except to say that it was something that needed to be let alone.

"It's not an easy thing to talk about," she said. Her face was turned away form me and her voice was soft. I had to struggle to catch the words.

"I can imagine. At least I hope I can."

"No, not like that. I'm not embarrassed. It's--like, for seven years I've been able to pretend that I've always been this way, that it had never been any different, and now I can't pretend anymore."

I waited. I knew now that I wouldn't need to prod her any further.

"Did you ever want something you couldn't have?" She was still looking away and her voice was muffled.

"Sure."

"I mean, not a thing. That you wanted to be someone else than who you were." She turned away from the window and looked at her hands in her lap. "When I think of my early childhood, all I can think of are my sister and my mother. Dad was never around. When he wasn't working he stayed away from home a lot. He and Mom hated each other. And even when he was home, he stayed inside his shell, never talking to anyone, just reading the paper or watching TV and biding his time till he could get out of there again.

When he died I was sad, but it didn't change anything because he'd never really been there."

She smiled sadly and played with a small ring on her little finger. "I don't blame him. It's no one's fault. It just is. But anyway, Lisa and I played together all the time; we were always close. When I was a baby she and Mom would dress me up in Lisa's baby things and she'd use me as a doll. When I got a little older, maybe three, they started dressing me in the clothes she'd outgrown. I know it seems strange, but it didn't then. I didn't understand about boys and girls; all I knew was that Lisa was my sister and we did everything together. And we were happy. From my earliest memories I associated playing with Lisa, just us two girls, with being happy." She paused. "And even then, I must have thought of myself as female. If I hadn't it wouldn't have seemed so natural."

"Lisa, you don't have to tell me the details if you don't want to."

For the first time she looked at me, and there was anger in her eyes. A lifetime of anger thrown back at everyone and everything that had made her life so difficult. What I saw wasn't some middle-class irritation. It was the raw rage of the woman who'd shot a man in the kneecap and would have done more if she'd had more bullets. "Damn it, besides my doctor and my mother, you're the only person in the whole world who knows or who will ever know. And you're not going to get out of this car thinking I'm pervert or sickie or something. Do you know anything about this kind of thing?"

"No."

"Then you start with the two-minute program on nomenclature. There're three reasons why a man would wear women's clothes, and they're different. A gay man might like to wear women's things-
-well, for the same reason women do, to attract men. Just like gays, or straights even, dress up in leather. It's a costume thing. The evening is over, and the costume gets put away. It has nothing to do with identity. Then there are transvestites, straight men who are turned on by women's clothes. They like women, and just like most men they like seeing women in sexy clothes, but they like wearing the clothes themselves, too. But they think of themselves as

straight with a kink. And then there can be a man who doesn't wear women's clothes to attract gay men--because he's not gay. He doesn't wear them because they turn him on. He does it because it seems right to do it. Because he knows he's really a woman and that the body doesn't make any difference."

She cleared her throat and went on. "The first time I remember that I really understood something was wrong was when I went to school. Kindergarten. Mom bought me some brand-new jeans. I hated them. I hated the boys being separated from the girls and having to stay with the boys.

"Lisa let me wear her underpants to school, under my jeans and it made me feel better. Like, I may have to pretend on the outside, but I can be me underneath. Mom knew about it; she must have. She did the wash. She never said anything. At home I still shared clothes with Lisa. But I understood that people outside the family weren't supposed to know about that. I learned to be ashamed. What was wrong as far as I was concerned that I had to pretend to be a boy."

"Things got a lot worse when I got to be a teenager. I started growing, my voice changed. I never had much hair on my chest or arms, but the little I had, I hated. I found myself changing into something strange. I used to think that if I avoided certain foods I could stop it, like they were poisoning me and making my body do these things. And in gym, I had to learn to be more careful about my underclothes. Once I got caught and beaten up. They said I was a fairy; I didn't even know what they were talking about. Anyway, Lisa was older, and she let me share her things--bras and slips and stockings. I'd wear them on the days I didn't have gym, and at home. And it felt so good; it was me. Putting on male clothes, I felt like one of those medieval knights putting on armor--it was ugly and clunky and uncomfortable, but it was something you had to do to protect yourself from the world. The only good thing about dressing like a man was how good it felt to get the clothes off again."

"It must have been complicated."

"You don't know the half. I had my gender issues, but I was as rebellious as any other teenagers and you can guess how mine came out. Around sixteen, I started dressing up completely, and going out in public. Lisa taught me about makeup, and I bought my first wig. At first, I'd just go out with Lisa for a drive. Then I'd go for walks late at night by myself. I was careful not to walk around our own neighborhood. I felt good and I felt ashamed at the same time. Then Lisa and I started going shopping; that was fun, especially buying clothes. The more I went out dressed up, the more comfortable I became. And the better I got at it. There are a million little things that men and women do differently. And I don't mean the obvious ones, like the pitch of your voice. It's how you sit, how you walk, the way you hold your elbows, gesturing." She smiled. "Let me tell you, the walking part is hard. Women's hips don't go from side to side because they decide to do it. It's natural. Their hips are wider and the whole center of gravity when they walk is a little different. I had to work at it. But by the time I was out of college, I could pass in any situation. At one point I even took a part-time job as a salesclerk as a woman. It was a good time. I had a circle of friends, strictly off-campus people, who knew me only as a woman. And we don't call it cross- dressing. It's *en femme*."

"I like the sound of that. It sounds natural."

"Of course, that goes back to the days when I moved back and forth." There was a wistful tone in her voice and I realized she was talking about an old part of her life. She wasn't *en femme* anymore.

"What did your sister think?"

"She accepted me. In a way it had always been that way. Going out into the world *en femme* was something new but it was just going outside with the way I lived inside. Sometimes she said she was sorry for me, that my life had become so complicated, but we joked about it, too. It wasn't all serious. We were siblings and we argued and teased each other like anybody else. Sometimes someone would call for Danny and I'd be dressed en femme, ready to go out, and I'd be talking on the phone about the Flyers or something in my masculine voice. Then the next night someone would call for Danielle-- that was the name I used then--when I was in man's clothes and I'd have to use my feminine voice. It always cracked her up. I liked to think that the joke was on the world, not on me."

"What about your mom?"

Lisa was relaxed now, just telling the story. The ice was broken. I wondered how many times she'd been tempted to open up and held back instead. I hoped our talk was doing as much good for her as it was for me. "You're going to have trouble believing this, but we've never really discussed it."

"If you don't know what to do or say, I guess you say nothing."

"She'd see me coming and going, sometimes dressed as a man, sometimes as a woman. She never said anything to me that she didn't say to my sister. Like, will that be warm enough, it's too icy for heels, that skirt is too short. No difference."

"How did that make you feel?"

"When I was a teenager, of course it made me mad that she never wanted to talk. I wanted confrontation. Now that I'm older, I understand. She's a first-generation immigrant with an eighth-grade education and she never leaves her house except for work or shopping. She doesn't have the tools to understand it. Practically nobody does. You ought to read the nonsense in the psychology journals. It worked out that she gave me the freedom to be who I am. And that how I feel about myself is up to me."

"When you were in practice, you were dressing then, and you had a blond wig."

"How did you--" she started, then stopped. "Someone saw me."

"Harrison, the black guy with the eyepatch across the street. He was fooled. And I think he was looking you up and down closely. Living in that neighborhood, you kept your expenses low. What did you do?"

"Some of my money I saved. I traveled with the rest. When I was out of town, I could live *en femme* without having to look over my shoulder."

"Do you wish it was different?"

"That, David, is the sixty-four-thousand-dollar question. I spent years in counseling, and that's the one way it helped. "

"Go on, if you want to."

"I've come to the point where I can talk about this in a dispassionate way, like I'm talking about someone else, and describing it from the outside makes it sound so neat and tidy. But that's not what it felt like. When you have a problem like mine, you go through phases. Sometimes you accept yourself and sometimes you think you're really a sick person. You purge your wardrobe. When I first started going out en femme, I used to feel very conflicted. That's a good old-fashioned psychological term for it. I'd feel great in a way, that the real me was getting out; and I'd feel like a jerk, too. There were times I hated myself as much as any ignorant fag-basher could have. When I was in that kind of a mood, I really hated myself."

"What happened?"

"Those moods didn't last long, and they finally stopped. And when I call them moods, I mean just that. It wasn't carefully thought through. The feelings weren't based in any facts at all. From my earliest memories I always thought of myself as feminine. The dressing up as a child wasn't forced on me. I wanted it. The games I played with Lisa made it easier, but they weren't the cause. Later I came to see that my moods were like growing pains; the masculine personality was dying as the feminine side took over completely and it didn't go down without a fight. That's why they started and why they stopped. I don't know if that makes any sense to you. It's hard for anyone else to understand."

"It's all new to me."

"At least you're not being condescending."

"You were explaining about your mom and your sister."

"What counseling showed me was that I had to make a basic choice about how I was going to see myself. If I was no good, a loser, a freak, then I ought to hate myself and blame my family. But if I felt good about myself, there was nobody to blame because nothing was wrong. It's a matter of accepting yourself."

"That part must have been hard."

"At fifteen, or twenty, I couldn't have done it. Accepting yourself is never easy, no matter what they are or how old you are. I'm not going to tell you that if I'd had the choice I would have wanted it this way. I used to think, why couldn't I just have been a normal guy? But that's thinking like a victim-- 'Why did it have to be me that got cancer?' I'm past that. And in one way, I was lucky. I was fairly short for a man, with a thin build, not very muscular. I could make the change and be convincing. What if I'd been six-five and two hundred fifty pounds?"

"On Saturday morning, in my office, you complimented me for being a strong person because I accepted responsibility for cheating on the bar exam. I've got no right to take compliments from you. That's peanuts compared to this."

"It's what you have to do. One of my counselors told me, when I was having a bad day, that I ought to go complain to the person who issued me a warranty at birth, guaranteeing that I'd live to be ninety, in perfect health, and never have any problems. I never felt sorry for myself again."

"Did Leo Strasnick know?"

"God, no. No one outside the family knew. And now there's just Mom."

"Did you ever try to tell anyone?"

"When I was younger. I was dumber then. I thought people just might be understanding, or at least tolerant. It would always go the same way; I'd start out with a remark about cross-dressing, something neutral, maybe about something in the news. The response was how they couldn't believe anyone could be sick enough to do something like that. I'd say something more, they'd talk about how the goddam queers were taking over and molesting kids." There was a pause while she thought about all the times she'd tried, and failed. "Then I'd give up."

"You never told Elizabeth."

"If there's anything in my life I really regret, that was that relationship."

"Regret?"

"I was using her, and she didn't know it."

"I've met her. There was plenty of that coming from the other direction."

"I started seeing her on my counselor's recommendation. He said that before I took an irrevocable step I should try once more."

"Let me guess. He told you that going out with a woman a little on the aggressive side might help."

"It just turned out that way. For a while it was okay. There was nothing wrong with her as a person, and I was lonely. But once we started having sex, I knew it wasn't going to work. There was nothing wrong with her physically, and I liked her well enough; I just didn't want to do it. I had to force myself. I realized, once and for all, that I wasn't attracted to women any more than any other straight woman would be."

"You started ducking her by going out of town on weekends again."

"You know what I told my counselor? It came out by accident. 'It's such a relief to get out of town and be myself.'"

"The money in the safe deposit box was for a sex change operation."

An edge of bitterness crept in. "We call it sex reassignment."

"Sorry."

"After three years I thought I might have enough saved, so I went to Johns Hopkins. Lots of fees, lots of forms, interviews, psychological assessments, personality profiles, MMPIs, medical exams, blood studies." She made a face.

"What happened?"

"Nothing. They told me to get counseling to help myself adjust to being a man. I said I'd done that for years. Sexual orientation isn't something you think through; you just have it. They said to go and get more counseling. Maybe take drugs to make myself feel better about my male body. They told me I wasn't a good candidate for surgery anyway. Ready for this? I was too normal. Stable personality, no delusions, not suicidal, coping adequately with society. They told me I didn't need it."

We both let the silence stretch out, letting it all settle. "I guess the only other thing is to tell me what really happened."

"You were right about everything between Strasnick and me. He took the money; he said he'd be putting it right back. For the good of the firm, he said. I was concerned, but I had no idea they were really after me. I thought if I pulled out of the firm I could put everything with the mob behind me. I was about to give Strasnick my formal notice of withdrawal and get a fresh start. I'd even drawn my money out of the bank. I'd made up my mind to have the operation, even if I had to go out of the country. Lisa was in town; we talked about the operation. She was very supportive--she knew how long I'd been thinking about it. My plan was to live with Lisa in LA for a few months as a woman, take hormone treatments, and then have the surgery. I was going to use the time to think about what I was going to do next. Whatever it was going to be, it wasn't going to be working for the mob any longer. Anyway, like I said, we went shopping. I was going to need some new clothes, everyday things, if I was going to live *en femme* at the time. They must have followed us all day, like you said, waiting to catch us alone."

"You were *en femme*."

"Of course. We were two girls shopping for clothes. I don't know what they would have thought of that—maybe they assumed it was a disguise. I guess they thought if I had really stolen the money, I would try to disguise myself. If they started following me from my apartment, following my car; they knew it was me. Anyway, I was driving north on Ten when a car pulled alongside, but it didn't pass. The passenger started shooting. The rest is just like I told you, except Lisa was the one who was slow in ducking not me. I'm sure she never felt a thing."

"You got to a phone, called your mom, and called it in."

"And I didn't call the police until after Mom arrived and we'd talked about it. She got there two hours later and we went back to the car."

"By that time you had a plan."

She nodded. "It sounds so cold-blooded now. But I was still in shock, my mind was working but I was all numb inside. And I knew that nothing--could bring Lisa back."

"You went back to the car and moved the body."

"I hid her a distance away in the woods where she wouldn't be found right away."

"Then you drove to the police station in your mom's car. Where was your mother?"

"At the McDonald's at the Morgantown exit. There was no way to explain her being up there."

"And you gave your statement in the car instead of inside because you were afraid you'd be detected."

"I'd stopped at a convenience store and bought a razor and some shaving cream. It had been fourteen hours since I'd shaved, and I wasn't on any hormones then. I cleaned up as best I could at the McDonald's. I stripped off my makeup and put on fresh. I tried hard to comb all the glass out of my wig. I knew I'd be a suspect. They'd look at me as closely as they could. But Dietz was basically a pretty nice guy about it, and God knows I didn't have to fake being upset."

"And then?"

"It was time to say good-bye to Lisa." She put her head down again but she didn't sob. All the tears had been cried a long time ago. "Mom and I had talked about it. If they thought I was dead, I'd be safe; if they knew they'd killed the wrong person they'd be back and she would have died for nothing. So I would take over her identity. We couldn't let the body be found. I had her wrapped in a blanket. There's an abandoned quarry, I think it was for limestone, for a steel company, a few miles away. I knew about it because the gatehouse had been used as a drug drop by some of my clients. The quarry was flooded, the water must have been a hundred feet deep. I wrapped her up as carefully as I could and said good-bye. That's where she is."

"She would have wanted you to do it."

"Thank you. I like to think so."

"Not just hiding her; I mean, pretending to be her. What happened to her gave you your chance."

She looked into my eyes. "I—I don't think many people would look at it that way."

"You do."

"You shouldn't be able to know that." She looked away.

"You make me feel naked."

"I thought that women liked it when men empathized."

"We do." There was a little flicker of a smile. "It's just . . . this is too much too fast and in the middle of everything else that's going on. For seven years my life never changed at all and in a weekend . . . But you're right. Ever since it happened, I've felt that my life has been a gift from her, and that it worked out . . . I was raised to be a good Catholic. I try to see that there's a higher purpose to all of it and I'm still trying. I feel it wasn't all a coincidence, but I've never gotten beyond that. I'm sorry I snapped. You've been patient with a long story and you deserve better."

"Tell me what happened next."

Lisa didn't want to linger. "The next thing was the operation. There's a clinic on an island in the Caribbean, Curacao, that does them purely on demand; no screening or waiting. No insurance. Cash on the barrelhead. I'd thought of going to them after Johns Hopkins turned me down, but I hadn't been sure before. I was scared I'd wind up with some butcher who didn't even speak English. But they were very good. The problem was me, not them. Most patients come in after months or years of hormone therapy. I came in cold. And I needed a lot of depilation in a hurry."

"Depilation?"

"Hair removal. The hormones help, but the facial hair and some of the other body hair needs to come off by electrolysis. It hurts when you do a lot at a time; I would sit through two sessions a day, as much as I could stand. It hurt more than the surgery, and that hurt a lot especially when I started moving around. They did breast implants, they said they were guessing about the positioning because the hormones would change my body shape. They came out a little bigger than I wanted. I also had them cut down my Adam's apple. There's a word for the operation but I forget. Later I had a nose job. It's funny; my nose was fine when I was a man, but after the hormones took hold it was too big. But that was a long time later; I'm getting ahead of myself."

"The hormones were to help your breasts grow?"

"It does a lot more than that. It makes your skin soft; it eliminates most of your body hair and changes the distribution of what's left. It changes around the fat distribution. Men carry their extra weight in their abdomens; women carry it in the thighs and hips. It changes your voice. But the main thing it changes is your personality."

"I don't understand."

"How you cope with stress. A man's testosterone is always pushing him, making him aggressive, wanting to fight. You take that away, and you can think so clearly. It's like you've spent your whole life with someone shouting in your ear urging you to pick fights, and then they shut up. The silence is wonderful. If something goes wrong now I may cry a bit, but then I pull myself together and solve the problem. I don't feel any urge to grit my teeth and start World War Three. Want to hear a story?"

"Sure."

"After the operation, after all the treatments, when everything was done, sometimes I would go to Common Pleas in Philly and watch my old friends try cases. No one ever recognized me, of course. Watching them was a hoot. There'd be a simple case, easy enough to settle, but one or the other--or both--of the guys would want to prove how tough he was. They would rationalize about why this or that principle was important, and why the case had to be tried. But what it really came down to was, they were all being led around by their balls. The testosterone said, 'Fight,' and they fought. They're just cavemen with briefcases. There's really been no progress in a million years. 'What do you mean, settle? I can try this! I'm hard! I'm ready! I'll show you!' She laughed. "I don't mean to go on and on, but it's such a relief being able to talk to someone."

"Go ahead, if you want."

"The doctors wanted me to stay in Curacao for two weeks. But that would have made the police suspicious. I was the closest thing to an eyewitness and now that some of the state police lab tests were back, they wanted to re-interview me. Mom was running out of excuses. I gritted my teeth and came back in five days. The hormones hadn't taken hold and the depilation wasn't a hundred percent complete, but I knew I could pass. I took some pain medication and got through it."

"I know this is a hell of a question, but any regrets?"

She laughed. "Only when I have to wait in line for a public restroom." Her smile faded a little and she leaned back in the seat. She closed her eyes. "Let me tell you about my flight back. I was traveling as a man, with a fake name. It was a good thing I didn't need a passport because Lisa and I didn't look enough alike that I could have used her photo. I went down dressed as a man and coming back I had to dress as a man. I hid my breasts by bandaging them flat and wearing a floppy tropical shirt. They weren't this size then; remember this is before the hormones. The plane changes got screwed up and I was in transit almost fifteen hours. It was stinking hot when I cleared customs in Philly. It was the middle of the night. My incisions were still draining, and I was so tired I could barely see straight. I was airsick, and my face was raw from depilation. I found an empty women's restroom, took in my suitcase, took off my male clothes and threw them in the garbage. I remember thinking, I never need to dress like that, ever again. I unbound my breasts and put on a bra and a summer dress and sandals. I tried to put on a little lipstick, but I couldn't--I was so happy I was sobbing uncontrollably. As hot and tired and sick as I was. It had all been a bad dream and finally it was over. That was how good it felt to finally be me after thirty years of living a lie."

"That's a hell of a story."

"And that's the way I feel this minute."

We were both quiet for a time after that. Then I looked at my watch; it was time to talk business again.

"You couldn't practice law and you certainly couldn't be a scrub nurse, so you took this job."

"Earning money wasn't important. I had enough to pay cash for the house in North Carbon, even after the surgery and the travel. Living up there helped me keep a low profile as far as the mob was concerned. I had to stay clear of anyone who knew my sister, of course. When I went out to Los Angeles to ship her things back and close up her apartment, I didn't try to fake it. I told her neighbors I was her cousin."

"That's why there are no old pictures of either one of you."

"Mom and I had to throw away a lot of things. I didn't dare keep anything, of mine or Lisa's, that could give it away. We never knew when someone might check up on me. That's why I brought back all her Spanish-style furniture even though it looks like hell. And why I faked some old photographs of myself as Lisa. And I threw away my glasses and got contacts that made my eyes darker."

"You did a thorough job."

"The toughest one was the graduation photo from nursing school I had to make it good enough for people to recognize me and accept it as legitimate. But remember, it's supposed to be a picture of a girl of about twenty-two. I was a good ten years older at that point."

"If that was the only thing, it would have fooled me."

"I kept my hormone pills with me, so you wouldn't see them if you found an excuse to come nosing around."

"You covered every angle you could."

"Then it was something about my body."

"Why do you say that?"

She became very serious. "I'm very self-conscious about that."

"There's nothing wrong with your body. Absolutely nothing. No one could suspect from that."

She dropped her eyes. "I don't really like asking questions like this. But my whole life has been about passing. Thank you for the compliment. Now tell me, how did you know?"

"Sometimes when the facts don't fit the theory you have to bend the facts. Why hide the body? The mob wouldn't have done that; they want people to know that they kill people who cross them. Someone else hid it. Again, who? Which gets you to why. I was stuck until I figured it out you'd been in the same car. Then I realized the killers could have hit the wrong person, you said so yourself. There's the why--hide the body to conceal the fact that the body isn't that of the intended victim. To protect the intended victim."

"That takes you as far as Lisa is dead and Daniel must be still alive. It doesn't tell you that I used to be Daniel."

"Someone fooled Dietz by appearing to be Lisa. Your mom could never have pulled it off; she's too old. It had to be you."

"Okay, it shows I masqueraded the one time, nothing more."

I shook my head. "If you had to do it once, it meant that you had to follow through or the whole thing would come out. Once you'd decided to play it that Lisa was alive, and Dan was dead, you couldn't very well have Dan reappear. I couldn't have known about your background or that you'd go as far as an operation, but I knew there was something wrong with your story even before I figured out that the wrong person was shot. Just as a start, why would a single young woman with a career go from Los Angeles to coal country?"

"To be closer to home?"

"Home is Philly, the better part of three hours away. And there are lots of nursing opportunities in a rural area that your sister could have taken advantage of, but you didn't, because you couldn't."

"You suspected before you went to my house."

"Saying that gives me a hell of a lot more credit than I'm entitled to. Let's just say I was puzzled."

"What did you find that convinced you?"

"I wasn't convinced even then. Maybe a little more puzzled. But to answer your question, it was what I didn't find. Like no tampons. And how many people don't have at least some childhood pictures of themselves and their family? Not one shot of Dan and Lisa together. You cleaned house too thoroughly."

"I went to a lot of trouble to fake the pictures that were there."

"The pictures that you did have around the place threw me for a while. Everything nicely documented. But when I thought about it later, I wasn't so sure. It looked too pat. Especially after I thought about how much Dan was into photography."

"How did you know about that?"

"Elizabeth. And the guy across the street from your old apartment. And your photography club in college."

"It's a common thing among people with a gender issue. I used to take lots of pictures of myself en femme. To reassure myself, somehow. It's hard to explain. But after the surgery there was no need."

"You cleaned house with Lisa's friends, too. Not everybody has a million friends, but not to see any of your old friends in seven years?"

"But none of that is enough. Tell me, there has to be something about my body."

"You keep asking that and I'm going to keep saying no. That part, I wasn't just fooled, I was impressed."

That one got a smile. "I'll shut up."

"It was a lot simpler than that. It's easier to hide your sex than who you are as a person. It was how you acted. Little things, like when we met the first day, you initiated shaking hands a couple of times. Women don't do that very often. They wait. You were careful to choose your words, but every so often you'd use a word that wouldn't come naturally to a nurse. When we were at your mom's apartment you talked about a 'limited purpose. ' "

"Anyone could say that."

"Sure, but we both know it's a term of art in evidence law. It's something Dan would have known. At your house you said, 'burden of proof.' And in the car, you talked about 'perjuring' yourself."

"And I thought I was doing such a good job of playing dumb with all my questions about law."

"You were good, but there was more to it than that. You didn't know things an experienced nurse would know. You didn't seem concerned about whether I had a concussion. I haven't had time to check it out, but the more I think about it, I think your advice about aspirin was wrong. It can cause bleeding. But there were other things. You talked about 'stitches' instead of 'sutures,' and you took my pulse the wrong way. You put your thumb on my wrist, not your first two fingers. The thumb has a pulse of its own, so you should keep the thumb away from the inside of the wrist. Anyone with any nursing training would know not to take a pulse that way.

But except for that you faked it damned well. If I hadn't been hurt I might never have made the connection."

"So last night--"

"No, I didn't know then. I still thought you were hiding him, I just couldn't figure out where or how. I hadn't made the leap yet. Want to know what really gave it away? Something simple, once I thought about it. When I was at Elizabeth's house she showed me a letter Dan wrote to her. The handwriting looked familiar. I figured there must have been a sample of Dan's handwriting in the file. But when I thought back, there wasn't. It looked familiar because I saw your handwriting on that questionnaire you filled out in my office."

"You're good."

"I'm an idiot. I can't see things at the end of my nose. I had the key to solving the case right in my hand Saturday afternoon and it took me until Monday morning to appreciate it."

Her voice was soft and very sad. "I'm glad you didn't realize it then. I'm glad we had last night."

I started the car and watched the gauges to avoid looking at her face. "It's almost time."

For the moment there was nothing more that had to be said. We rode without talking. I think both of us were grateful for the silence. A lot had been said, on both sides, and it was time to reflect.

I dropped her at my office and headed for Strasnick's office.

CHAPTER FIFTEEN
Monday, 11:00 A.M.

The same fashion model was at the reception desk, but this time she was wearing a drop-dead black dress with a gold pin. There wasn't much time to look; she had hardly finished announcing me before Strasnick burst in and hustled me into a small conference room. He was wearing the same jacket, still without a tie. His complexion was terrible--white and blotchy at the same time. His hair was a mess and his eyes were bloodshot. He still looked better than I did. We sat across from each other at a small table inlaid with at least four kinds of wood, plus gold leaf. Even if it was a reproduction, it must have cost more than all the furniture in my apartment. I didn't want to think what it was worth if it was an antique.

Strasnick leaned forward, trying to keep his voice low but not quite succeeding. "We have a problem. There's—"

"What do you mean, 'we'?"

"Cut me a break, Garrett."

"Like you cut your partner?"

"The money's all here. Look." He picked up a briefcase from the comer and pushed it across the table at me. I opened it. Money bulged out, in every denomination and description: bundles of brand-new five-hundred-dollar bills, still in wrappers; rolls of hundreds in wrappers; and handfuls of hundreds lying loose.

"It's all there," he repeated eagerly. "Go ahead, count it."

"I'm going to, believe me. These people aren't going to take being shorted." I started to count. "Now, what's the problem?"

"My firm. We had an emergency partner's meeting just now. They won't go along with paying off Wilson's estate."

I let him sit till I'd counted all the five-hundred-dollar bundles and put them in a stack to my left.

"Then you're going to have to raise the other hundred thousand yourself, too."

"You can't mean that. A chunk of what's here comes from the sharks already. I'm going to need to give them a grand a day just to pay the interest on this."

I rummaged through the case, segregated the bundles of hundreds, and counted them. out. There were a lot of them.

"Ever occur to you that all this started with money that wasn't yours to begin with? I mean, if you put fifty grand in the bank for seven years, it turns into a hundred. All you're doing here is giving back what you stole, with a fee to me for saving your ass. You got off real cheap."

His mouth trembled, and I could see his hands shaking.

"This is *it*, Dave. I did everything you said and more. There isn't another nickel!"

The counting slowed down even more on the loose hundreds, but when I was done, the count was exact. I didn't look up at him once. The money was in neat piles across the table. I counted off twenty thousand in five-hundred-dollar bills for myself and to pay Louch's fee and marked it with a big paperclip. Then everything went back into the case. It was a few minutes before noon.

"This thing's a package; the one-twenty and the one hundred for the life insurance. I'll tell you what I'll do, Strasnick. I'm going to give you thirty days to come up with the other hundred. If I don't have it, I'm going back to the counselor with you."

He had no way to know if I was bluffing. Neither did I.

Sweat broke out on his forehead. "I told you--I can't do any more. I'm leveraged like crazy. I was, even before I had to come up with this."

"In thirty days you can sell your house if you knock the price down enough. That place has got to be worth the better part of a million."

"But-I-"

"Take a hundred off the market price, hundred and a quarter. If you can't get to settlement within thirty days, the broker will buy it from you and hold it for resale."

"With the loans against it I don't know if there's a hundred in equity! I'd sell it and have nothing."

"Let me tell you what it means to have a partner, 'cause you don't know. If you can't stand your partner either you dump him, or he dumps you. But as long as you're together, you play it straight with him. Absolutely straight. You can cheat on your wife and bullshit the judge and stay drunk every minute you're not working, and it's your own business. But when it comes to your partner, you go hungry instead of hitting the petty cash for lunch money if that isn't part of your deal. Because no matter what else goes on, you need to be able to count on each other. But you--you did worse than leave him alone. You sent them out after him and left him to die. I'd love to give you right back to them. I'll tell you, I'm sorry I even need to give you a chance. It's more than you deserve."

He looked into my eyes, begging. If he was looking for pity, there was none to be found. "You can't leave me with nothing. I'm almost forty. I've got a wife and two kids. I can't start from scratch at my age."

"Then I'm not going to make the delivery. And it looks like you're going to die."

He pulled back from me, folding his arms across his chest and hunching over, as if he were trying to roll himself into a ball. He closed his mouth tightly and looked down at the table. For a long time, he didn't say anything. "Okay," he whispered at last. "You'll have it."

I picked up the briefcase and opened the door. He was still in his chair, his head bent. I don't know if he knew I was still there. There was something dead in his eyes. I put my hand on the knob. I wanted to leave, to put as much distance us as I could. But I couldn't just walk out, like a delivery boy on an errand. What Strasnick had done, what had happened in this room, what was in that briefcase, was important. It deserved a moment of its own.

One person had been killed and another forced into hiding because of what I was carrying. Now another life was in shambles. Three lives had been changed forever by the money. Four if you counted the man in the ditch. Five if you counted what it had done to me. The case felt heavier in my hand.

I looked back at him. "It's over," He turned his head, but his eyes looked through me. "It's been a long time, but it's finally over. All your work, your practice, your clients, everything you've built up is gone. It might as well have never happened. You're back where you started. And you know something? You're the lucky one."

He focused on me briefly, then his eyes glazed over. Down the corridor I could hear a female voice laughing softly. The sound might as well have come from Mars, there was nothing to smile about where I was. My world was about wasted lives and trying to patch them up as best I could. I shut the door behind me.

My ride whisked me to an abandoned warehouse in Camden where the money was counted out by three men in total silence. I pocketed my twenty thousand and met Lisa back at my office. She was sitting where she'd sat for our initial interview a hundred years ago. She stood up like she wanted to throw her arms around me, then stopped. We looked at each other awkwardly.

"It's done," I said. "It's all over now."

"Really?"

"You never need to worry about this again."

"I don't know what it will be like, not having this hanging over my head."

"It will take a while to adjust."

"I hope that now you can tell me the rest of the deal."

I was glad for a chance to focus on business. "From your point of view, it's simple enough. I bought amnesty for you and Strasnick. Or rather, Strasnick did, for both of you. He returned the fifth thousand plus another fifty as a penalty. Plus he paid my fee, and your attorney's fee. Strasnick will be honoring the buyout provision, so you'll be getting the hundred thousand within a month."

"They won't be after me?"

"That was part of the deal."

"Do they know I'm alive?"

"They know Dan Wilson is alive. Even though that's not true."

She looked at me and I watched emotions play across her face. She couldn't decide what she thought. "You--listened. To everything I said."

"I'm trying to understand."

"I liked what you just said about Dan." She was still processing. "The hearing is off?"

"Permanently. There's no need since Strasnick is going to pay it out of his own pocket. I have to call Mark and tell him. And I should probably send a bill to the life insurance company. I did a hell of a day's work for them."

"And for me. Thank you. And thanks for listening to my rant."

"Do you know what you'll be doing now?"

"Two weeks in Cancun. I've been dreading this hearing for a long time and I promised myself a big treat when it was over, one way or the other."

"No, after that."

"Haven't decided at all. I'll be making some decisions while I'm on the trip, I guess."

"You know, with the organization not after you, there's no reason why you can't practice law again."

"Are you serious?"

"Not as Dan Wilson, of course. But Danielle sounds fine. Or any name. You could even use Lisa, I guess. You can get a change-of-name hearing done discreetly for a couple of hundred bucks. No judge would say that you should be required to go through life as 'Dan' now."

"If I don't have to hide who I am--Jesus, you're right. But what kind of a firm could I get into? I can't explain the last seven years. Or why I can't give them references for the five years before that."

"Forget the firm route. Hang out your own shingle. You'll have a quarter of a million dollars as seed money. And you'd be a hell of a family law practitioner. Or a criminal lawyer, if you can get the men to trust a woman. Or whatever you want to be."

"You're giving me a lot to think about."

"Let me give you some more. Lisa's dead, but you're the one who's been buried. You've wasted some of the best years of your life in that little town. Until now you could kid yourself that you had to hide out. That excuse is gone now. You've done enough penance. It wasn't your fault."

We were quiet for a moment, trying to set a new footing now that our business was done. Then she looked up. "I need to get you back to your car. And I need to see my doctor about this hand. Can we take a little side trip on the way?"

CHAPTER SIXTEEN
Monday, 4:00 P.M.

The gravel road was in poor shape, and my side complained at every jolt. The underside of the car brushed over weeds, bushes, and even some saplings. Rivulets crossed the road, washing away what little gravel remained. At the rate it was eroding, it would be hard to find the road at all in a few more years. With a few inches of snow, it would be invisible even now.

About half a mile after we turned off the last paved road, we came to the rusting, twisted remains of a sign: BETHL- the rest was illegible. A few fifty-five-gallon oil drums, equally rusty, were scattered about. Farther up, we came to a half-collapsed shack. The windows were broken out and the door was missing. A PRIVATE PROPERTY-KEEP OUT sign hung at a crazy angle, shot full of holes.

Lisa pulled behind the shed and parked. "Want to come along?"

"I'd like to, if it's okay with you."

She opened the trunk and pulled out the floral wreath we'd bought in King of Prussia. It was big, almost four feet in diameter and she was having trouble with it in the wind. I stood aside and tried to break the wind a bit; with my ribs, I was in no position to help more than that.

The ground ahead was open, except for some brush and saplings. The day had clouded up and turned colder since noon. The wind, gusting at unpredictable intervals, made it hard for me to keep my balance. I stayed on her windward side and concentrated on keeping my feet.

"Here we are."

In front of us was a wide expanse of dark water, big as a lake, ringed by gray stone slopes on all sides. It was hard to see the far side in the failing light. The water, sheltered from the wind, was blank and unruffled, as still and dark as death itself.

"I used to come here a lot," she said after a while. "Not so often anymore. I'm not sure why I come. I was raised Catholic but as far as whether she's here or knows that we're here, I don't know. Maybe it's just easier to focus my thoughts here."

"This is better than a cemetery. They're full of grass and flowers and inscriptions to cheer up the living. They're prettified and phony. This is how it should be. It's a dead place. A place for the dead."

"It's her place." We looked out across the water. The wind stung our eyes. "Ready?"

"If you are."

She was ready to throw the wreath by herself, but I stopped her. "Let's do this together."

"But your side."

"I'll use my left arm."

Together we threw the wreath over the edge. It bounced once on the slope below us, then rebounded into the water. There was no splash.

We both stood, watching, as it slowly sank out of sight, on its way to join Lisa on the dark and rocky bottom. When it disappeared completely, she turned to me. "What are you going to do, once I get you back to your car?"

"I'm not going to take any cases for a while, in my condition. All my bills are paid. I was thinking of a vacation." I watched her face. "Maybe a couple of weeks in Cancun."

Her eyes opened wide and her face turned scarlet. She lowered her face and shook her head furiously. "I would never have told you all those things if I thought I would ever see you again."

"You were truthful, and honest."

"I've spent my life just trying to be what I really am, and I've spent the last seven years trying to forget the first thirty. After I transitioned, I swore that if I ever met a man I liked I'd never tell him the truth. I couldn't stand to have him look at me like I was a freak."

"I don't."

"But you know," she insisted. "How could you want me?"

"For the same reasons I'm attracted to women who are smart, and tough, and sexy, and good-looking. No difference."

"That's easy enough to say."

"I'm looking you in the eye, knowing everything, and I'm telling you that it's fine with me. Who has the problem?"

"We can't pretend it's not there. Not anymore, anyway."

"I can accept you, the past and now. The question is, can you? Remember what I said back at the car this morning before I left, when I dropped you off?"

"About how you wanted to see me again?"

"I meant it."

"You knew then," she said. Her voice was barely audible. "When you said it."

"And everything I said to you last night. Knowing doesn't change anything."

"It's crazy. The odds are so against it."

It was my turn to laugh. It wasn't loud, but it seemed to echo around the quarry. "They always are. You can't let that stop you."

It was a long time before she answered. "It's been a long enough day already. And there's a long way to go."

We stood there a moment longer; then the wind picked up and snow started to fall. The water was as still and black as ever. We walked back to the car and drove away.

THE END

I hope you enjoyed the first book in the series. Here is the first chapter of the second:

THE FEBRUARY TROUBLE

CHAPTER ONE
Monday, 6:00 A.M.

I LIKE THE TIME JUST before dawn, when the sky begins to lighten. When I was a kid I used to get up when it was still fully dark. I imagined it wouldn't be just the sun starting to shine on the same old things—I had a fantasy that each time the sun came up, the world was created out of the darkness, from scratch. I waited to see if it would turn out the same.

After Nam and the ambush and the hospitals, after I was off the medication, I'd drink all night and wait to see if things might be different. But my squad never came back and every morning the scars were still there.

Later still, the summer after my divorce, I was up before dawn again. I wasn't drinking much by then, just sitting in the backyard in a lawn chair, thinking and waiting. Hoping that one of those dawns, things would be different, that I would be able to go into the bedrooms and see the kids that had never been born. Once, while I was prowling the hallways, I thought I saw them, a couple of little blonde girls snuggled in bunk beds in a vacant room. I never looked again.

"Mr. Garrett?" It came from my right, in the shadows next to a dumpster. A young man's voice, cheerful and energetic, a man who hadn't seen nearly as many dawns as I had. I stepped back and put down my briefcase to free up my hand. He stepped forward under the streetlight. Late twenties, well dressed, clean shaven, and bundled against the cold. Not many people who worked around my office looked much like him. The heck of it was, even in the dark and cold, he looked happy to see me. I couldn't imagine why.

"Who are you?"

He stepped closer and I moved back, maintaining my distance. This was not a block where surprises were ever good.

"Hi, Mr. Garrett, I'm Larry. Larry Bonner. I've been waiting for you."

He extended a hand, but I didn't take it. "I don't think I know you."

He dropped his hand to his side and kept on smiling. It was going to take more than my refusal to shake to put a dent in his mood. I wondered why he was so confident. I kept my eye on his hand, but he kept it there. I stayed on the balls of my feet, my knees slightly flexed. "No, sir, you don't. I've been sent to offer you a job."

I watched his eyes. If he was getting ready to make his move, he was good at concealing it. His body was relaxed, and his feet were firmly planted. Either he really meant me no harm, or he was very, very good. I played for time and said the first thing that came into my head. "I just got back from vacation." He stayed still. "I'm still on vacation till tomorrow."

I looked past him, over his shoulder, watching the shadows. Then, without turning my head, I looked quickly to both sides. Street eyes, the cops call it, always in motion, always watching as much of what's going on around you as you can. In the neighborhood where I worked, you needed them. But it seemed that we were alone. I settled back on his cheery face and wondered what came next.

"This is an emergency, Mr. Garrett. A serious emergency. We'd like you to consider starting right away."

"Who's we?"

"Can we go inside and talk?"

"Here is fine."

"I've been freezing my ass out here. And I don't want to talk business in public."

"Not unless I frisk you."

"If that gets us out of the cold, no problem."

"Turn around. Open your coat and extend your arms out to the sides."

Once I had him facing away, the first place I checked wasn't him, it was behind me. There was nothing but broken sidewalks, abandoned cars, and the dark bulk of row houses and storefronts. The streetlights glinted on dirty snow and broken glass in the street. The usual stuff. As far as I could tell I was as safe as I could be in this neighborhood.

I patted him down, front and back, all the way to the ankles. I checked the pockets of his jacket. There was no gun, of course; he wouldn't have let me search him if there was. Mainly I was interested in how he reacted to being touched, and he passed the test. He was ill at ease. Nobody likes being touched by strangers. I wasn't going to risk being alone with someone who was used to being frisked.

I unlocked the two front door locks, threw back the dead bolt, and pushed the door. It didn't move easily; when it had originally been fitted, the builders hadn't allowed for the weight of a one-quarter-inch sheet of steel. Just inside was a small foyer with a grimy black-and-white tile floor.

A dozen or so pieces of mail addressed to the various tenants were lying there, left over from Saturday, but I didn't bother. Sorting and delivering it would give the receptionist something to do with her day. Probably all there would be to do.

I relocked the door behind me and took Bonner up the stairs to my own office. I made him go first. My door had a double lock of its own. My mail had been slipped under the door but otherwise the room was the same as I'd left it, two weeks before. A file cabinet, chairs, and a desk, all secondhand. The file cabinet was mostly empty except for a stack of paperbacks I read to pass the time between clients.

I motioned Bonner to one of the chairs. He unbuttoned his coat, looked around for a hanger, then shrugged and threw it over the top of the filing cabinet. When he sat down I saw a fine puff of dust rise off the cushion. Damn those cleaning people anyway.

I found a yellow legal pad and uncapped an Ace Check Cashing and Notary Service pen. At one time Ace had maintained an office upstairs, but when his second rent check bounced, the landlord changed the locks and put his things out on the street. They were gone in half an hour of course. Ace worked out of his house now, and his line had expanded to include crack and numbers.

"You said 'we,' Mr. Bonner."

"Uncle Chan's."

"The fast-food chain?"

"Franchise," he corrected. "The fastest-growing one in the country. We've opened three stores in New Jersey in the last thirty days, with ten more planned for this year."

"I'm not licensed in New Jersey, and I don't know the territory."

"No, no. This is local. The work is for our franchisee for south-central Pennsylvania. Chadwick, Bruce Chadwick. He lives in Lancaster. We've had problems with the new restaurant. Vandalism, every few days. Some serious stuff, as far as cost is concerned. Between direct and indirect costs, we're out more than fifteen thousand dollars already. We've had warnings not to open the restaurant."

"Have the police been notified?"

"Just on the initial problem, with the windows. Not as far as the rest. If that's what you recommend, we'll do it, I guess. But you can discuss that when you meet our franchisee."

"Not so fast. Just who are you?"

"Chief administrative assistant to the head of the Middle Atlantic Division, Corporate. "He made it sound like he was chairman of the Joint Chiefs of Staff, but I let it pass. He was entitled; he was half my age and probably made twice as much as I did.

"This sounds more like a site security job."

"We've already got some rent-a-cops. If you have suggestions to improve security, we'll listen. But mainly we want you to find the source."

"How did you get to me?"

"We think you're uniquely qualified. If I've got my facts straight, you have management experience in fast food."

"If you count a few months as assistant manager of a Taco Bell, yeah."

"You know the business. It counts for something."

"How did you know I was even in town?"

"My boss is Bob Mosier; he's head of operations for the whole Middle Atlantic. He's in Lancaster now, helping Chadwick get the first restaurant open. He told me to locate someone. I made some calls and got your name. Found out you were in Cancun till Sunday. I waited. I got here at five.

I didn't think there was much chance you'd show at the office any earlier."

"It can't be twenty degrees out there."

"My boss doesn't like to hear excuses."

"You couldn't have had any idea I'd come by this early, or even that I'd be in today at all."

"If you didn't show, I would have gone to your house."

"You don't know where I live."

"If I needed to, I would have figured it out. I have a job to do."

I couldn't see why he wanted me, but I liked people who weren't afraid of hard work. I wasn't interested in the job, but I decided to hear him out. "Tell me about this guy."

"Bruce Chadwick. He was business manager for a corporation that operated a dozen Holiday Inns. We're lucky to have him." He paused. "We're hoping you can meet him this morning."

"You're relentless."

"We've heard you're very good."

"Then you know I don't have to scramble around for every piece of business I can find." I'd made a nice fee off my last case, and even after the overdue bills were taken care of, my checking account was in five figures. It wouldn't be there long--I needed to give some of it to Uncle Sam, and my Honda was going to celebrate her tenth birthday soon, but for the moment I was free not to have to take on some strange out of town trouble that walked out of the night into my office. And I was still trying to figure out why they wanted me so badly.

"We know that, Mr. Garrett. We'll pay five hundred a day, plus expenses. I have authority to give you a thousand-dollar retainer right now. And if the case resolves in less than two days, keep the change."

"I still haven't said I'll take it."

"But you're interested."

"I'm interested in lots of things. But not all at the same time. Besides, this sounds like something for the police, or a security company if you want this kept private."

"My instructions are to hire you."

I didn't feel like walking into a union mess or trying to break up a protection racket. Or much of anything that required a lot of energy, just then. Last week had been the twenty-second anniversary of the day my platoon was ambushed, and each year it got worse. I wasn't sure I was up for a project like this. Or maybe I was plain scared of it.

"The city of Lancaster has a fine police force; your man doesn't need me."

"I'll make you a deal. Come to Lancaster; talk to Chadwick and Mosier. If you still think there's nothing you can do, tell them so, call the police, come right back here, and keep the thousand." He put a check on my desk.

"I don't take sucker money."

"I'm serious. Look, my job is just to get somebody there. Whatever happens from there, it's off my desk. It's not my money."

I fingered the check in my hand, trying to decide exactly how much trouble it represented. He saw me still hesitating. "Look, give this some thought. I know you're tired but come out and see at least. If you don't, I froze my ass for nothing."

He said it as if it meant something, but it didn't. I was tired in a way that had nothing to do with sleep or travel. Cancun hadn't been about sun. It had been about two weeks with Lisa or what should have been two weeks. We had only met a short time before, but that hadn't mattered. I found myself caring for her more each day and for a while it was reciprocated. Very reciprocated. For ten days it was as good as it gets. And then, like the flip of a switch, it was gone. Lisa went to sleep loving me and I woke up in the morning to a silent stranger wrapped in a sheet and staring out the window. I spent two days trying to get her to talk. Finally, I flew home a day early so we wouldn't be in the same plane. I'd cared for her when it was good; I didn't know exactly how much till it went bad. Just then I didn't have a lot of sympathy for either Bonner or his ass, no matter what its temperature. I folded the check and stuffed it into the breast pocket of his shirt. "Sorry, I'm not available."

"My boss will be disappointed."

"His expectations were too high."

He seemed about to say something, and then caught himself. "Then I guess we're done here."

Part of me was relieved to get rid of him and part was sorry to see him give up. I was getting used to his pestering. "Sorry you made your trip for nothing."

"Thanks for hearing me out." He didn't sound thankful. He handed me a card with his cell phone number as he stood to leave. "Give me a call."

The office was agreeably quiet without him. I didn't know how long I was going to need to lick my wounds, only that it was going to be more than a day. Lisa was special. Lisa was the first person who'd made me think about the long term since . . . well, my first wife, and that was a long time ago. There were people who threw themselves into their work to get away from their personal problems, but I wasn't one of them, at least not any more. All I wanted to do was stay still. I'd been hoping to sit quietly in the office, no one around, and be still. It was something I was good at and it was something I needed.

There was no newspaper yet, and there was nothing of interest in the mail. My answering machine was by my desk. I rewound it and set it to play. A lot of messages had accumulated. A couple were from prospective clients; more were from existing clients calling about their cases. One was complaining about her bill. The building superintendent at my apartment had called; all carpeting was being replaced; please call and set a date for installation. The next call was from my lawyer; the state supreme court had refused to reconsider its decision disbarring me. There was nothing more he could do--he was sorry. A final bill would be forthcoming. Two calls from the body shop; they were ready to fix the old dents in my Civic whenever I could get it down there.

A phone solicitation for magazine subscriptions. And then one from a voice I didn't recognize.

"Mr. Garrett, sorry to have to bother you with news this way, but it's unavoidable. And I don't like leaving a voice message but this is urgent. This is Michael Fletcher at the operations center of First Pennsylvania Bank. We've just received a court order from the US Attorney's Office in Philadelphia freezing the twenty-thousand-dollar cash deposit you made several weeks ago. I can tell you that this is a RICO order, that the government thinks the money could be from organized crime. I've checked with our legal department and they assure me we need to honor this.

Please understand that the money is still there--just we're not allowed to honor any checks against it until this matter is resolved. And by the way, there was a check to a Mark Louchs, Esquire, which we had to dishonor in the amount of four thousand dollars. I'm very sorry to have to give you this news. Feel free to call in and speak to our customer service representatives."

I stared at the machine. They were sorry? Not half as sorry as I was. The check to Louchs was only a part of the problem. I wrote a check to cash to cover the fee of a snitch I'd used to break the January case. And in celebrating my success I must have spent three thousand of the rest, between the airfare and the hotel and meals. The hell of it was, I'd earned that money. Earned it the hard way and now it was gone because some GS-12 hit a button on a computer. Two minutes ago, figuring that five of it had to go for taxes, I'd been eleven or twelve grand ahead. Now I was three or four in the hole. Or maybe eight or nine—for all I knew, the government would want me to pay taxes on it. I wished I'd been a tax lawyer. Or a ditch digger. Anything other than a private eye with money problems.

I looked at the answering machine. It looked back. Louchs would get his money, one way or another. I would figure a way to make the check to the snitch good, if it hadn't cleared. That part of it was just money. The part that had been spent on Lisa . . . I wish I could say that I was glad to have a job with guaranteed payment, but I wasn't. All the reasons for not taking it were still good. The only difference was, I didn't have a choice.

I picked up the phone and dialed his cell. It went to voicemail; I'm sure he was busy reporting back to his bosses.

"Tell your boss I'll be out there this morning." I didn't give him a time; it was all the independence I had left.

Made in the USA
Las Vegas, NV
29 June 2021